# CA$H IN
# CA$H OUT

ASSA RAYMOND BAKER

GOOD 2 GO PUBLISHING

**CASH IN CASH OUT**

Written by Assa Raymond Baker

Cover Design: Davida Baldwin – Odd Ball Designs

Typesetter: Mychea

ISBN: 9781947340336



Published 2019 by Good2Go Publishing

7311 W. Glass Lane • Laveen, AZ 85339

www.good2gopublishing.com

https://twitter.com/good2gobooks

G2G@good2gopublishing.com

www.facebook.com/good2gopublishing

www.instagram.com/good2gopublishing

# CA$H IN

# CA$H OUT

# CHAPTER 1

On a dimly lit block just off of Villard Avenue, Max's search for a parking space ended when he observed a little white Saturn leaving the parking lot. He quickly slid his freshly washed, dark green Chevy Cruze into the slot between two fully tricked-out big SUVs. From the look of the packed parking lot and street in front of Bonkerz Gentleman's Club, Max could tell he had made the right choice of strip joints to shop in for a date. He was not looking for a wifey; instead, just something sexy for the night.

After making sure his gun would be easy to reach if he needed it, he then exited his car. He could still not believe the steal he got on the used Chevy he had gotten from a woman on Craigslist earlier that day. With the woman being a hype and Max a young D-boy, she sold him the car for three Gs and five grams of crack. It was filthy inside and out, it was badly in need of an oil change, and its front windshield was badly cracked. But Max had taken care of all those issues as soon as he got it home. The young thug had gotten released from the house of corrections about four months ago and was starting over from the bottom. Not one for hard work, Max got up with one of his guys and started hustling crack to support himself.

At the entrance of the club, Max paid the ten-dollar cover charge to get inside and found the place jumping, just the way he had imagined it would be from all the stories a few of the older inmates in his cellblock had told him. There was action going on with sexy and scantily-dressed strippers in almost every corner that he looked. Max made his way over to the bar with his eyes locked on the girl-on-girl performance taking place on the cash-littered stage with a colorfully lit runway that projected from it. Max could not wait to join in on the action. Once he got to the bar, he flagged down the barmaid and ordered a double shot of Hennessy and two cold MGDs, along with two hundred $1 bills to start off with for the night.

His goal was to find a whore that was willing to

go to a motel with him by the time the $200 was gone. Max knew that was not going to happen as soon as a phat, colorfully tattooed ass was bouncing and clapping in his face. The dancer quickly reduced his wad by $50 before kissing him on the cheek and moving on to the next horny guy waving cash in her face.

When his second beer was half empty, Max's attention was called to the stage by the live house DJ just before dropping a hot remix to the hit song, "Bottoms Up." A big-titted Latina with pale green, blond, and brown hair came tumbling down the runway like she was Gabby Douglas; only her tumble ended in the splits, with her firm butt bouncing wildly off the floor.

A hot exotic beauty simultaneously materialized at his table and asked, “Would you like a dance?”

“What, from you? Hell yeah! And while yo’ at it, tell me what else I can pay for,” he said while licking his lips as he took in her curvy shimmering body.

“Don’t I know you from someplace outside of here?” she asked once her hips started swaying to the music.

Before he could answer, her honey-dipped hips dropped down, and she slowly brought her butt up before dropping it in his lap.

“I doubt it! A nigga could never forget some-thing as fine as you, ma. But what’s yo’ name anyway?” he asked with a handful of her ass.

“Champagne, but I’m sure that I know you from

somewhere else. I don't forget many faces. What's your name or what do they call you?"

She dropped into his lap again, rolling and grinding her hips on him. As she danced, she could feel his hard-on pressing on her thigh through his jeans. Max loved the way Champagne had him feeling. He avoided answering her by stuffing small stacks of singles in her tight, pink lacy bottoms and bra strap.

"Can we get a room?"

"Sure, it's $25 to start," she told him before she then looked over in the direction of the VIP rooms and saw one with its light off, which signified that it was available. "If you want it, we better hurry, 'cause one's open right now."

"That's not the kinda room I'm talkin' about, but I'll take whatever from you."

"Oh, okay. You gotta keep that down. I can get in some shit if somebody hears you being all reckless and shit. But, yeah, we can if you willin' to wait until I get off work. We're not allowed to leave once we get here," she explained, now off rhythm with her dance.

Suddenly, a fight broke out between a butch-looking dyke and a dancer two tables over from them. Before Max could agree and confirm the time, Champagne was up on her feet and moving as the DJ asked everyone to sit down and the girls to line up on the back wall next to his booth. This gave the bouncers time to get a handle on the situation.

When it was over, Champagne was nowhere to be seen, so Max found a pretty-faced, extra-thick girl with big legs and a monster ass on her to take to fuck on for the night. She only wanted something to smoke, $50, and a ride home—in that order. Somehow Max knew he probably would have gotten the same deal with the goddess he was hitting on first. He also knew he would not have been fucking her in the back seat of his car the way he was now doing his cheap-ass consolation prize.

# CHAPTER 2

Early the next morning, Champagne was dropped off at home by the club owner, Scrap. It was a moniker he was given by his guys because he was always collecting things. Scrap was also Champagne's unofficial boyfriend. She let him claim her because he had money and took good care of her. But he had a mean side that Champagne had witnessed many times in the club and a few times firsthand. But Scrap only lost it when he was drunk and upset at somebody that owed him money and could not pay, or with her if he thought she was spending too much time with a customer in the club. That is why she continued to live in her own place instead of in Scrap's nice downtown condo overlooking Lake Michigan that he owned and had offered her the keys to many times.

Champagne lived in a big four-family house in the front lower unit. She noticed a shadow of someone standing on the side of her place in the gangway and went to investigate while Scrap was still there. What she found was Max's familiar face talking to a crusty-looking man that she just knew was a crackhead. She wanted to say something to Max, but before she did, she knew it would be best to let Scrap go on about his business first.

"Champ, what's good? Is everything alright over

there?" Scrap asked, getting out of his black Cadillac DTS that was sitting on 24-inch black Davin Pearls.

"Yeah, I just thought I heard something. It's okay! It's just them in the back, so you can go," she told him while pulling out her keys and unlocking her door. "Bae, make sure you call me when you get back."

"You know I will," he promised before he got back in his car and pulled off.

Champagne went inside, kicked off her heels, and dumped her club bag in the dirty clothes hamper before taking a shower for the second time that morning. She knew she had seen Max before. It was when he was moving into the lower unit behind hers. She was not quick to place him so close to home, because she only went back there to park her car for the night and to take out the trash. She did not see him much, but she had noticed all of the in-and-out traffic he had going on, which could only mean he was doing some type of hustling back there.

* * *

Max was sitting in his kitchen chopping down ounces of freshly whipped crack into grams, so he could bag them up and get some much-needed sleep before his next rush. He had been up ever since he dropped off the chubby chick at her home after he banged her outright in the far corner of the club parking lot. Max was in a zone and bobbing his head to Lil Boosie's hard lyrics until he heard someone knocking on his door. He snatched up his gun and went to see who it was. He already knew it was not one of his hypes, because they all knew to use the remote doorbell he had hidden on the far end of the back gate. He did this so non-costumers would not use it.

"Yeah! Who dat?" he yelled, at the same time looking through the peephole.

"Hey, it's Champagne. We kinda met at the club last night. I told you I knew you from somewhere."

"Yeah, okay! So how ya know where I live?" he asked in surprise when he saw her.

"Oh, I live in the front unit."

Max opened the door, hid his gun behind his back, and blocked her view into the house so she would not see the drugs out on the table.

"Okay, ma, what's this visit for?"

"I saw you kinda working on yo' car yesterday and was hoping you could see if you could get my key out of my ignition. I don't know what happened, but it won't come out, and I don't want nobody to steal my car. Can you please come and try to get it out for me?" she easily lied, playing the damsel-in-distress role.

Before she knocked on his door, Champagne went and knocked her maroon Kia Sportage out of gear. She knew it would not allow her to remove the key unless it was firmly in park.

"Okay, hold up! I'll see what I can do. I'ma be right out, so just give me a sec," he said before he closed and locked the door out of good habit.

He then put his gun and dope up just in case she wanted to let him hit that for fixing her car, if he could, that is, because he did not know much about cars. Max grabbed the small tool kit one of his hype buddies had traded him for some work a few weeks back and went out to meet her at her car.

"So, you fix cars?"

"Nope, just my own, I like to have things just so. Know what I mean?"

"Yeah, my Uncle Curtis is like that. It'll take a lot for him to throw things away or pay somebody else to do it. He's always trying to make things better. He just likes to tinker with shit."

"Woman, how long have you been drivin'?" Max asked as soon as he found the car was not in the right gear.

"Why? What is it?"

"You didn't have it in the right gear. Yo' ass was either really tired or high as a bitch to forget something like this. If it's the second one, let a nigga get a sack of that shit there," he joked as he handed her the keys.

"Ohhhhh, you saved me! I don't know what I would've done if I couldn't get this key out and somebody stole my car. Thanks! What do I owe you?"

"It's all good, unless yo' tryin' to continue our plans from last night?" he suggested, showing his gold-toothed smile.

"Ummm!" she said as she wet her lips and

returned the smile. “Yeah, we can do that. I’ma give you the good-neighbor discount,” she joked. “My place or yours?”

“Yours! I ain’t got a bed yet. Just a trusty air mattress,” Max lied, just wanting to see how she lived.

Champagne agreed, and he followed her ass to the front of the house. When they got there, Scrap was sitting on her steps smoking a blunt with two of his Murder Mob goons standing next to his DTS.

“Hey, bae, is everything alright?” she asked, shocked to find him there when he was supposed to be in Chicago.

“Who the fuck is this nigga? Is this the reason why ya ain’t answering my fuckin’ calls?” he asked as he stood up, which caused his two goons to move closer to Max while just waiting for Scrap to say the word.

"Yeah, he is. But it's not like that. I couldn't get my key out of my car, and he fixed it for me. So, chill with that jealous shit! Dang!"

Max hated that he did not go back for his gun right about then. He knew if Scrap did not buy her story, he was going to have to fight with them or a bitch he had not even taken down yet.

"Okay, bitch, but that don't tell me why you didn't answer yo' fuckin' phone or why you's about to take him in this house?"

"Scrap, I forgot my phone and stuff in the house. I was worried about my car. I was just finna pay him for fixing it. Now ya really would've been mad if you had to buy me another one 'cause somebody stole it."

Champagne glanced at Max. She hoped that he would just go along with her story and not get on no tough-guy shit with Scrap and his guys.

Scrap seemed to notice for the first time that she was not carrying one of the many expensive designer bags she loved so much for him to buy her.

"Champ, you know how I get. I worry 'bout you; so, when you walk outta the house, make sure you got yo' phone with you. Do I gotta tie it to yo' hand for you to remember?" he tried to mask his threat to her as he pulled a large wad of cash out of his pocket and peeled off two bills. "Thanks fo' lookin' out for my bitch, my nigga. Here, I hope this is good enough for yo' trouble."

Max took the $200. It was obvious to him that Scrap was just trying to show him that he was a boss.

"Yeah, it's good. Champ, make sure you have Uncle Curtis tighten up that gearshift." He flashed his smile at her before he then returned back the way he had come.

He was not at all disappointed by not being able to get between Champagne's thick legs. Just knowing that she was so close made him believe it was going to happen when the time was right.

# CHAPTER 3

It had been a few days since Champagne's encounter with Max. She found herself looking for him to show up at the club night after night, but he never did. She began to wonder if he was avoiding her because of Scrap. She was sick of Scrap chasing her friends away, and she was not going to let it happen with Max. So, before she went into work, she left a note on his car inviting him to the club.

Little did Champagne know that Max wanted to see her just as badly.

Max hated to feel like he got punked in front of her or anybody else. The only reason he walked away was that he knew he had to be cool while he was still on paper. In fact, Max found the invite on his way in to see his probation officer, Ms. Munday. She was not like most other POs with whom he had worked in the past. Ms. Munday was drop-down fine as hell. She looked more like a hot video model than a stuck-up state representative. Max did notice that Ms. Munday was much friendlier to him than how he witnessed her with a few other parolees. She seemed to genuinely want Max to make it outside of a cell. She never really tripped on him not having a job. She let him be as long as he did not miss a scheduled visit with her without first calling and he kept up with his monthly supervision fee.

"I'm glad you're here on time, Max, because I have a meeting to get to that I can't be late for," Munday told him when she walked out to greet him in the office lobby.

"What! Ya couldn't have just called me and told me you was gonna cancel on me?" he asked while standing to face her. "It's Friday, so I bet your so-called meeting is to get yo' weave done," he joked with a big grin.

"Don't do me, Max. This is not a weave! It's all mine; and, no, I couldn't have called, because I'm not one of yo' little airhead girlfriends. You just be glad I like you, or I'll be sending your ass to the county for the weekend for coming at me like that."

Max did not know if she was joking or serious.

"I was just joking about all that, Ms. Munday! Damn!"

"Yeah, I know. I just wanted to see your reaction to me getting on you like I do my others," she said with a smile that showed her dimples. "Now that we got that out the way, walk me to my car. Max, you've been doing so well on your supervision that I'm making this our last office visit. Well, you'll still have to come in to sign out on your last day, but this is it."

"Oh snap! That's what I'm with right there." Max showed his excitement as they walked to the parking lot.

"Don't get happy just yet. I'm making one last home visit sometime next week. And I'm coming in this time, so have that little shack of yours cleaned up."

"Okay. Can I know what day, so I can have the red carpet rolled out for you?"

Ms. Munday stopped in front of her shiny silver GMC Acadia.

"I'll think about it." She smiled again. "Max, just stay out of trouble for a few more days and get off this paper. You got a whole life in front of you. I'd hate to see you waste it in a cell."

"I got you, Ms. Munday, 'cause I got me."

He hit the remote start on his car that was now fully restored.

"Is that yours?" She pointed her French-manicured finger at his car. "See, it's little stuff like this I could get you for, Max. Not telling me you bought a car!"

"I just got it, and I was gonna tell you today, but you rushing to get to yo' meeting, remember?"

"Okay, when I do my home visit I'm going to need to see all the paperwork," she said as she looked up after admiring the 22-inch rims he added to the car, only to see Max pull out some rolled-up papers from his back pocket. "Not right now, Max! I got to go, unless that's my copy to keep?"

Munday liked the fact that he was not lying to her about telling her about the car.

"No, I need this, but I'ma have you some when you do your home visit," he promised.

When she agreed and climbed behind the wheel

of her SUV, Max strolled back to his car, got in, and pulled out behind her. He then turned in the opposite direction so as not to have her think that he was following her.

The thought of getting off probation did not seem real to the young thug. It would be the first time he ever made it through without messing up and getting locked up. For him it was reason enough to celebrate. Max looked down at the note from Champagne and knew he would be doing it at Bonkerz; and if all went well, he would be celebrating balls deep in her. As he navigated his way through the busy Milwaukee streets, he imagined how good it was going to feel having Champagne all over him while giving him a lap dance.

# CHAPTER 4

Scrap was interviewing a new girl in his office at the club. But he already knew that she was a good dancer, since she had been working at the club for the past few months. This interview had nothing to do with that. Scrap wanted to know if she had what it took to be a mule for Murder Mob's drug operation. Scrap had just made the twenty-one-year-old, petite, big-titty white girl strip down to nothing but her heels in the room full of his goons, when something caught his attention on the monitor.

He watched as a member of Murder Mob got a

lap dance from Champagne and was being a little too touchy-feely with her. Scrap did not mind her doing her job. In fact, he loved to watch her dance. This fit of anger that was building was not because of her; it was because of the clear disrespect from whom Champagne was dancing. Scrap knew Champagne knew who the guy was, and that was the only reason she had not stopped the dance. He was sure of it when he witnessed her slap his hands away a few times when he got a little rough even after knowing who she was and who she belonged to.

"Hey, Badman, finish up here! I need to go handle something upstairs."

Badman knew that whatever was going on, it had

to have something to do with his girl.

"Hold, my nigga! What ya wanna know about this bitch?"

"Hell! Strap her up and see how she moves with stacks taped to her. I need to know what she'll do under pressure," he instructed before leaving to go upstairs with two of his other men with him.

* * *

Max strolled into Bonkerz with one thing and one person on his mind. After examining the lust-filled crowd inside, he found her on the far wall giving a lap dance to a thugged-out dreadhead who seemed to be really trying to get his money's worth out of the dance. Max could tell from the frown on Champagne's face that she was not enjoying herself, so he decided to step in and once again save the day. That was when her boy toy showed up with a couple of his buddies and one of the bouncers from the door.

The big bouncer snatched up Dreadhead from his seat like a rag doll, and then he and the other two men walked him out of the club. He saw Champagne exchanging a few hard words with her guy before she marched off to the dressing room. After what Max had just seen, he made his mind up to see her another time. Tonight, was not right to make his move on his beauty. He wondered why her boyfriend let her work at a strip club if he could not stand to see her do her job. But little did Max know that Scrap owned the club and was pretty much there with his eye on Champagne the whole time.

"Hey, you, I thought it was you standing over here. Can I get a dance or are you here for round two?" the chubby girl that hooked up with Max on his first night in Bonkerz asked.

Max turned toward the eager-to-please whore.

"I wouldn't want ya to get in no trouble 'cause I'm about to leave," he said to her, remembering Champagne telling him that the girls could not leave once they arrived at work.

"Man, fuck them! It's been slow for me tonight with all these new bitches, and a bitch needs to smoke. They won't miss me. So, what's up?" she asked, with her long colorful fingernails gripping her wide hips.

Max did enjoy her wet shot, and after all, he was trying to celebrate.

"Fuck it. If ya down, let's hit it. I'ma be in the car rollin' up. If ya ain't there by the time I'm done, I'm out."

"Wow, that's how ya gonna rush a bitch? Can I get a head start or something?"

"Yo' head start is me finishing my drinks!"

"That'll work. Are we getting a room this time? I wanna show ya how good this box really is," she said while dragging her hand across her gold boy shorts and biting her bottom lip.

"If I do, we pullin' an all-nighter! I don't got it like that to be fuckin' off. I'ma lil' nigga in the game."

"Yeah, right. Them Trus you wearing are saying

something different, but I can do all night as long as you get me home by seven."

Max agreed, and she rushed off to get changed to leave with him. Since he knew Kake was a cheap lay, he decided he would have fun with the three hundred $1 bills he got for his lap dance with Champagne, which was now not going to happen.

* * *

Max sat back in the cozy Super 8 Motel smoking on some fruity-tasting kush and drinking Crown Royal, which was a bottle Kake stole from the strip club on her way out the door to join up with him.

"Ma, I got all these ones I brought for the club, and now I'm not there. What you gonna do to fix this?" he asked, letting his eyes roam up her thick toned legs that ended at her short black jean shorts.

"I can give you everything you could've got at the club here, and some. How about that?" she asked while taking a deep pull of the blunt.

"That's what I'm talkin 'bout. Dance for me. I want a lap dance and everything. Put them sexy-ass heels on for a nigga, too," he told her.

Max then pulled out two large wads of cash from his jacket pocket that was draped across the arm of the chair next to the table on which he was perched.

"Oh, lil' daddy, it wouldn't be right if I didn't!" she said while pulling out her cell phone and turning on some music for her to dance to.

Max sat down on the edge of the bed waiting for the show to get started. Kake gulped down the rest of the drink in her cup and then put her heels back on. She then released her long, curly, honey-blonde-and-red weave, and let it fall over her shoulders and frame her face. Max had to admit she was sexy and knew how to move her body.

Kake started removing parts of her outfit as she ground her wide hips to Gucci Mane and Nicki Minaj's hit song "Girl After Girl." She was then rewarded by Max tossing small stacks of bills in the air over her head, so they could rain down on her. This was just as much fun for her as it was for him. Kake was not used to just chilling with a guy without him trying to put his dick in her mouth. She was soon clapping her big soft ass in his face, and Max loved it. He tossed all of the 200 ones he had all over her before he then held her by her waist and buried his face between her full titties. He lightly pinched one of her nipples while flicking his tongue over the other one.

"Oooh, daddy, take yo' clothes off! I wanna feel you on me," she moaned while holding Max by his head as he teased her with his tongue.

Kake pulled away and climbed onto the bed with her legs spread to him. She played with her clit as Max undressed for her.

Max first removed his shirt and let her see what two years behind bars looked like with his cut muscular upper body and six-pack abs. He then dropped his jeans, and Kake let out a moan like she had cum without him. Max quickly joined her on the bed and slid his thick fingers inside her wetness. While he worked his fingers in and out of her, at the same time he worked her clit with his other hand and sucked on her inner thighs.

"I need to feel you in me. Bring that big muthafucka up here so I can suck it before you slam it in me," she panted while clawing his strong shoulders.

"Nope! I want you to taste yo' cum on me when I decide to put it in yo' mouth," he told her before pulling her legs over his shoulders and pounding in and out of her.

Kake was not what he wanted to be balls deep in, but she was what he needed.

# CHAPTER 5

Not long after Bonkerz closed for the night, three of Scrap's goons went to work in the basement of the club. They were teaching one of their own a hard lesson in respect.

"Please, I'm sorry. Y'all don't gotta do me like this. I fucked up! I didn't know."

Badman hit him in the mouth before he could finish what he was pleading.

"You don't know what?" he screamed as he punched him again. "I hope you was finna say you didn't know that you's a stupid drunk. 'Cause if ya lie to me and say ya didn't know who Champ was, I'ma really fuck you up. You disrespectful to the bitch, boy."

They ferociously beat Dreadhead until his face was swollen and unrecognizable. Two of the three goons worked him over as their white tees were stained with his splatter. But they took a break when Scrap entered the room.

"Nigga, you had the nerve to put yo' hands on my bitch. What! You wanna take my spot. Ya wanna be me or some shit, huh, fuck boy?"

The barely conscious man could not answer because his jaw was clearly broken and badly swollen, which only infuriated Scrap more.

"Bad, I don't think he gets it yet. I don't want him

dead but just wishing he was, feel me?"

"Scrap, I'm already on it. Folks, snatch up his BM right now so we can show him how it feels to have a nigga all over his bitch in his face," Badman announced as he looked into Dreadhead's face. "Yeah, nigga, we finna have some fun with yo' bitch while you watch."

"Do what you do. Just make sure he knows his place from here on out!"

Dreadhead sprung from his seat as he tried to make a run for the door. One of the men thought he was charging at Scrap and shot him three quick times in the back and side, which instantly killed him.

"What the fuck!" Badman yelled while pulling out his own gun. "Fam, didn't you just hear folks say don't kill him?"

"Yeah, I thought he was coming for y'all, so I did what I had to do," he explained while lowering his gun. "And let's keep this shit real. We couldn't let that bitch-ass nigga live after what we just did to him. He was gonna get right up and try to get some get back; and if he didn't, we didn't need his soft ass 'round no way. Either way he had to go."

"Mike-Mike, that's why I keep yo' ass around. You always thinking ahead. Now get this shit cleaned up and call the others and tell them to leave his bitch alone. She don't need to know we had anything to do with this here."

"What if they already got her, then what?"

"Let her go. Tell her it was a mix-up and they

were supposed to be making sure she was alright. Whatever! Just don't kill her or give her any reason to put this on us," Scrap ordered before he then left them to get to it.

"Champ, I'm done here. You ready?" he asked as soon as he walked into his office.

"Yeah, I'm ready to go home. I'm not in the mood tonight. I just wanna go home, take a hot bath, and curl up in my bed until I gotta do this all over tomorrow night."

"Champ, I just handled that punk for disrespecting you, and ya not gonna at least spend the night with me? That shit's crazy!" Scrap said as he collected his things to leave the club.

"I was good, Scrap. Whatever y'all did to him,

you did that shit for you, not me. I'm not sayin' I'm not thankful that you got my back. I'm just sayin' I'm too tired to show you how much tonight," Champagne explained as she also gathered her belongings.

"Bitch!" he slapped her hard in the back of her head, so hard it almost felt like he had punched her. "I'm not the nigga to be begging a bitch to do shit!"

But just as fast as he snapped, his mood flipped, and he began to apologize for hitting her.

"I'm sorry, ma. I'm trippin'! I just wanna be with you tonight. I can't be alone tonight. It's been a week and some since I been with you. I miss you, Champ. We don't gotta fuck. Just come stay with me tonight, and I'll take you shopping when we get up."

Champagne was caught off guard by him hitting her. She knew she did not want to be hit again, so she agreed to spend the night at his place.

"Okay! Alright, bae," she said while letting him see her tears fall. She planned to make him pay for every last one of them. "I'll stay with you, but I got stuff to do in the morning. I wasn't tellin' you no or tryin' to make you beg me. I just hate to leave early when I'm with you. And I got an early time to get my hair done, or my hairdresser won't be able to fit me in until Monday," she lied.

* * *

Upon returning to his immaculate home, Scrap was going out of his way to make up for putting his hands-on Champagne. She knew he felt bad, because this was the first time he brought her to his house to spend the night with him. Scrap once told her that he bought the home for the woman he decided to take as his wife; so, until then, he used the place for a safe place to spend time with his daughters when their mothers let them visit.

"Come take a shower with me. Ya know I'm good at washing backs and other hard-to-reach places."

"Yeah, then afterward you can give me a real massage," she answered, not wanting to set him off again and cause him to hit her.

His soapy hands were all over her in the shower. She gave him what she knew he wanted. Champagne moaned from his kisses on her neck and breasts that he placed on her in between soaping her down. Soon his fingers found the way inside her silky folds. She took hold of his hardness with her soft and soapy hands, stroking him until he was unable to hold his fingers' rhythm inside her. Champagne knew just how he liked to be touched, and tonight she was going to give him everything he liked. She planned to make sure he cashed out on her for what he did to her, and she did not mind getting her hair wet to ensure that would happen.

She dropped down, took him in her warm mouth, and deep-throated him while at the same time massaging his balls. Then she slid her fingers back to his opening. When Scrap did not push her away, she felt his thickness jerk in her mouth. She pushed the tip of her finger into the hole while still giving him head and playing with her clit with her other hand. He then relaxed and let her penetrate deep inside.

Scrap moaned as he started pumping in and out of her mouth in time with Champagne's fingers sliding in and out of him. She did not know this side of him, and the thought of being in control of him was enough to make her cum shortly after Scrap filled her warm mouth with his load. She did not swallow, but she did keep sucking until he was drained and surprisingly still hard from the excitement of what she had done to him.

Champagne then stood bent over, so he could fill her twitching box from the back. Scrap roughly pounded deep in her just the way she needed him to. Spasms soon shot through her and made her legs weak as she came hard. For the first time in a long time, she did not have to fake it with him. As they lay beside one another, she was already thinking of how far to go the next time they got together.

# CHAPTER 6

Two days later, Max was behind his house helping his friend, Slugga, upgrade the stereo in the Cruze. Max wanted to keep the factory radio to throw off passengers when they got inside, so Slugga built onto it. He added a 1,000-watt PowerBass amp to power the six-speaker components, and a 3,000-watt PowerBass amp to power the two 15-inch subwoofers in a nice custom fiberglass box. The two men were just about to install the subwoofers when Champagne pulled into the slot next to them followed by a black-and-yellow

Camaro.

"What up, Tank! How come everywhere I'm at, you show up? Ya following me or something?" Slugga joked to the man who got out of the sports car.

"What's good, Slugga. I ain't following you, but I see I should be 'cause ya always seem to be where the money's at," Tank answered before he then followed the beauty into her place.

Max was a little envious of the six-inch Asanti rims that Tank had on his ride, but mostly his feeling came from wanting to be the one going into the house with Champagne. "Man, I gotta get my money up."

"Man, Max, yo' ass is gonna have to put in a lot

of work to catch up to that nigga. You looking at his trapper right now. Tank got like four or five whips that I know of that make one look like trash. I built the box for the Camaro and his BMW 3281," Slugga informed him while putting the finishing touches on the wiring before they could put the box in the trunk and be done with the project.

* * *

"Now, Tank, what's so urgent that you had to talk to me in person, and please don't say ya just needed to see me, 'cause I've got things to do," Champagne said once they were inside her unit. "I told you that I can't do this with you anymore. You friends with Scrap, and that nigga's crazy. If he finds out we been fuckin', he gonna kill you. It don't matter that it's business between us. Paying for it or not, all he is gonna see it as is disrespect, no matter what."

"Fuck that nigga, Champ! He's a bitch without Bad around him, and I'm trying to fuck with you on some real shit. I want you to pack up and move to Atlanta with me. Straight up, just take what ya can't live without and leave the rest. I'ma buy you all new everything."

"Are you serious right now? I can't just up and leave!"

Tank walked up on her, grabbed her hand, and placed a large roll of hundreds in it.

"This is to show ya how serious I am about this. I want you with me."

"I don't know," she said as she squeezed the

bankroll, not wanting to give up such an easy large sum of cash. "Do ya have to have my answer right now? Can I think about it?"

"Yeah, but I'm trying to do this ASAP. Can you let me know by the end of the week? I should have everything in place for us by then." When she agreed to have an answer for him by the end of the week, Tank smiled. "Take off yo' clothes, unless ya want me to rip 'em off?"

Champagne did not want to give up the money. So, she decided to give him a quickie, and did as he asked so he would not destroy her expensive Dolce & Gabbana outfit. When she was naked, Tank pushed her down on her soft sofa and then dove between her knees. He sucked and licked on her wildly, quickly bringing her to orgasm.

* * *

Max paid Slugga as soon as he concluded the work on his car. Max then ran into his unit to grab a sack of rocks, so he could catch the couple of hundred bucks his hype buddy had for him online. Once inside, he could hear Tank banging out Champagne next door. Max grabbed his work and gun before he went back out to get the money. Not wanting to go back inside and have to hear them again, he decided to go for a spin to test out his upgrade. He also decided to stop and get something to eat, hoping the Camaro would be gone by the time he returned.

Just as he turned out of the alley, Kake texted

him and asked if he could come through with something to smoke. With nothing else to do, Max told her he was on his way. He then let the hard lyrics of Gucci Mane's hit song "Hood Up" pound as he stormed through the streets on his way to pick up Kake and take her out to eat with him. Kake seemed to always be there when he needed her to get his mind off of Champagne.

# CHAPTER 7

The following day while driving down 27th Street, Champagne passed Max at the gas station on Wright Street. She was sick of him not talking to her, so when she made it the house, she sat on his outside step and waited for him to return. She did not have to wait long before the thundering bass of Max's car could be heard as he turned onto the block.

Max killed the sounds when he entered the alley behind their housing complex where they parked, and he then pulled into his space next to Champagne's car. He was concentrating on his phone when he stepped out, so Champagne had the thought to jump out and surprise him. But after catching a glimpse of his gun hanging out of his belt, she quickly discarded that idea. She did not want to get shot if he did not like the surprise.

"Hey, Max, how you been? I see you avoiding me," she said, standing up so he could see her in the dim light of the street lamp.

"Why you out here by yo'self? Oh, yo' guy Tank must've just left, or is you out waiting on yo' other guy?" Max asked as he found the right key to unlock his door.

"Why can't I just be waiting on you? And you didn't answer my question. Why are you avoiding me?"

"I'm not avoiding you; our timing just don't match up. I was at the club when you left the invite on my car, but then yo' guy showed up and I got into something else. I ain't tryin' to cause no shit between ya all," he explained as he entered his unit.

"Is you gonna let me in or you still embarrassed about not having shit in your house?" she asked, already stepping inside with him.

"Damn, don't give me a chance to say no and shit!" He closed the door and locked it behind her. "As ya see, I don't got shit to be embarrassed about up in here. I've did a lot since I told ya that shit."

Champagne was impressed with the neatness of his place. He had a lot of iron and glass. The dining room table was wrought iron and glass, and there were three tables in the front room that closely matched the one in the kitchen. He had a nice black leather seating area that consisted of two La-Z-Boy chairs and a sofa. The 42-inch television on the wall displayed a slideshow of him and his car and stacks of cash. Beneath that was a 75-gallon aquarium filled with little cheap colorful fish which she did not recognize. Champagne mostly wondered if he had gotten a bed yet.

"I see ya checkin' me out. I got a real bed now, too. I couldn't keep livin' like a bum and shit. Plus, it's cheaper to bring my company here than to keep payin' for motel rooms that go to waste when I don't stay the night."

"Did you do all this for me, for real? Come on, you can tell me," she joked with a big smile. "It looks nice up in here, and I can tell you did all this yourself. It's very manly."

"I don't know! Thanks. Now what's up?" Max asked taking in the way her yoga pants hugged every curve just enough to make his length begin to rise.

"Nothing, I just wanted to see you. I do still owe you, and I do plan on making good on it. I can't have you talking shit about me to yo' guys."

"What makes ya think I'm still on that with you? Hell, a nigga ain't tryin' to be into no bullshit with neither one of them lame-ass niggas I seen you with," he said before setting down his fish dinner that he picked up from JJ's Fish & Chicken on his way home from making a run to collect $300 from one of his hypes.

"Boy, stop! I know you still on it 'cause I'm that bitch. And if you wasn't, I wouldn't be in here with you right now. I know a real nigga from the rest," she said as she moved closer to him, opened up his dinner box, and plucked out a few fries. "I'm choosin'; and nigga, if you snoozin', ya losin'," she told him before taking a bite of the fries in her fingers.

"Never that! Ya lookin' at a winner, baby. Success is the only option for the thug. So, if ya really choosin', show me something I can believe," he told her before he popped a few fries into his mouth as well.

Champagne considered herself far from a dumb street whore. She sold sex with the best of them but did not put her money in anyone's pockets but her own.

"Okay, there's a first time for everything, and I'm all for treating myself," she said as she counted out $200 from inside the new Louis Vuitton bag she had bought from the money that Tank had given her the day before. "Here, call this a refund on what you spent at the club on that knock-off bitch, Kake. Don't look surprised. A big ass ain't the only thing big on that hoe."

"Hey, I was on some drunk shit!" Max told her, feeling the need to vindicate himself.

"I ain't trying to hear that shit, nigga. I'm just

trying to find out if your fuck game is as good as that bitch say it is. As you call them, the lames ain't hitting it right."

"Shit! That's not what I heard when that nigga Tank was hitting that."

"You can hear me?"

"Yep." He nodded and then smiled at her surprise.

"Was you jealous?" She returned the smile.

"No! Well, maybe a little," he admitted, showing his attraction for her.

"Well, don't be, because I was working. But I can't lie to you, that nigga's head game is the truth. He just can't hit my spot with that lil' meat he's packin'. Now, is we gonna do this or keep talking about it? I want you to give me something to talk about," she said, finishing off her fries and then washing them down with a bottle of cranberry juice she had with her.

Max could not believe she was really asking him for sex. He accepted her money and then went and put his food in the microwave for later. He watched Champagne watching him as she waited for him to make a move. Max wondered if Kake told her about when he asked her to dance for him. That night was fun, so he decided he would play with Champagne a bit before he banged her brains out. And to ensure that he did just that, Max popped half a Viagra to experience what all the hype was about and not let down his beauty.

"Max, let me run to my place right fast. I got some whipped-cream-flavored Smirnoff. It's good; you'll like it," she said as she walked toward the door and then answered a text on her phone.

Max locked the door behind her and got ready for when she returned, just in case she was on some setup time. He placed one of his guns under the foot of his bed, so he could reach it quickly if he had to. He put one under the pillow of the sofa where he kept it when he watched television and bagged up his dope. He then placed the pleasure pack of condoms next to the bed, so she could see them.

"This bitch better hurry up," he said out loud, starting to feel the effects of the drug.

Right then Champagne knocked on his door. He

peeked out the side window to make sure she was alone, and then again out the peephole before he let her in.

"Did I take too long for you or something?" she asked while walking inside.

Max noticed that she had changed into hot-pink yoga pants and a fitted shirt with no bra. She had also put her hair up in a ponytail. He thought she was still fine, even dressed down as she was.

"I was just about to eat my food while you were over there putting on yo' comfy fuck-me clothes."

"I just wanted to make it easy for ya. I don't want nothing in your way," she told him as she began to rub on his semi-hard length. She then purred and wet her lips. "I see you're working with something!"

"You don't know just how much yet, ma," he began as he took the Smirnoff bottle from her and poured two full cups. "Sorry, I don't own no dishes. Just paper and plastic."

Max rolled up some strawberry kush as soon as the smoking and drinking started, which was followed by some fondling. Max quickly had her on his bed. She was topless, and he then pulled off her pants. The drug had him on brick. He was so hard that all the games he had in mind for her went out the window. He needed to be in her so bad that it hurt a little.

Champagne took hold of his now fully hard thickness as soon as his pants came off. She stroked him as he sucked on her breasts, nipples, and chest. He touched her like he had touched her many times before. Nothing about it said, "new lover." She pulled him onto the bed, pushed him down, and straddled him. Champagne rubbed the tip of his hardness back and forth through her opening before she guided it inside. As soon as he parted her warmth, she knew she would not be disappointed.

# CHAPTER 8

Champagne arrived at the club early, so she could see why Scrap had been missing in action for the past few days. When she turned into the parking lot, she saw Badman's Audi A6 blocked in by two police cruisers, and the officers had him and another man she did not know in handcuffs stretched out on the ground. She picked up her phone and sent Scrap a text telling him what was going on outside of Bonkerz. He called back and instructed her not to say anything to them, and just to come inside the club. Champagne got out of her car with her work bag and made her way across the lot. As she passed Badman, he smiled and winked at her. That was when she noticed the guns and drugs displayed on top of the Audi, which were clearly the reasons for the arrest. She also noticed Tank's Camaro parked next to Scrap's Escalade, which was right outside his private entrance that led straight to Scrap's lower-level office.

* * *

Kake no longer charged Max for sex, but she always wanted weed when she called. Since she was his official go-to girl when he needed to get a nut off, he thought it was a fair trade. So, he purchased a few ounces of kush to save a few bucks instead of paying for a couple of blunts at a time.

Max was too busy with the last-minute rush of crackheads to put away the weed when his cousin, Amo, dropped it off to him. He was happy that things had slowed down that morning, since he only had gotten a couple of hours of sleep since he had found Champagne waiting for him when he got home.

Max was just stepping out of the shower when he heard a knock on his door. He glanced at the clock on the microwave, which read 8:15 a.m. Since it was still early, and due to the fact that the person was knocking, he guessed it was Champagne at the door. So, he pulled on some black Levis over his naked ass and then walked to the door.

"Yeah, yeah, yeah! Girl, lay off the damn door!" he yelled before he opened it without looking out first.

"Good morning, Max."

"Whoa! Hey, I wasn't expecting you this early. Give me second to put on some clothes, and I'ma be right out."

"Oh no! That's not going to work for me, Max! I told you I wanted to come inside when I made this visit," Ms. Munday said as she put her body close to his in the doorway, so he could not close it on her without hurting her.

"I know, but I ain't dressed, and it's kinda messy in here."

The parole officer placed her hand on her gun out of habit.

"Move and let me in now!" she demanded as she

forced her way inside. "Is there anyone else here?"

"No just me," he answered in shock that Ms. Munday had threatened him by exposing her gun.

He did not know what to do. He did his best to remember what was laying out in the open that could get him locked back up. He had his dope in a pizza box in the freezer, and he had a gun out on the sink in the bathroom.

"Ms. Munday, let me at least put on a shirt so we can get on with this," he said as he began to move toward the bathroom.

"Oh my fuckin' goodness! Really, Max?"

When he looked back to see what had surprised her, he saw her holding the large ziplock bag of weed. His heart skipped.

"So, this is how you've been buying all the nice clothes and that car?"

"No, I smoke that. I don't sell weed, Ms. Munday."

"Fuck you, Max," she yelled as her hand went to her gun. "That's the same tired shit all you mutha-fuckas say when you get caught. I believe in you, Max. I thought we were cool." She sounded more hurt than anything else to him.

"Ms. Munday, we good. I wouldn't lie to you about something like this. You can drop me right now. My pee's dirty. I got that there to smoke, that's it. On my life."

"Okay, mister. On my life! On *your* life! Can you explain these big bankrolls on the table next to it, huh? Wha, Max? What do you got to say about this?"

* * *

Scrap met Champagne at the door and practically dragged her through the empty strip club and downstairs past his office to the room known as the Adjustment Box. Inside, Man-Man stood over Tank with a baseball bat. He was just about to dispense another round of strategically placed blows to his body.

"Bitch-ass nigga, shut up!" Scrap yelled at Tank as he cried out for mercy. "Put something in his mouth. The police out there are locking up Badman and Tommy. The last thing I need is them hearing this punk screaming."

Man-Man picked up one of Tank's socks from

the pile of clothes they stripped off of him before the real beating started.

"Here! Put this in his mouth," he said as he tossed the sock to Goat, who was the other goon in the room, who stuffed it into Tank's mouth.

"Did y'all find out where he got the dope and money at?"

"Not yet, but I'm on it now that Bad's gone. I'ma make him talk to me," Man-Man promised before he slammed the hardwood across Tank's bruised back.

After leaving his two remaining goons to their task, Scrap took Champagne back to his office. He just wanted her to see Tank all bloody and beaten. Once they were inside his office, Scrap slapped Champagne.

"Bitch, you didn't tell me about this nigga!"

"Scrap, no, stop! I don't know what's going on. Please, baby, stop it!"

He slapped her again.

"So ya didn't know he wanted you to leave with him and that he was trying to take you away from me, huh, bitch?"

"No! I mean, yes! I was trying to call you to tell you about him, but you wasn't returning my texts," she lied. "It's why I'm here so early now. So, I can tell you about it and find out why you wasn't answering me," Champagne explained, with tears streaming down her red face.

Scrap's temper softened after hearing her tearful explanation.

"So, you wasn't gonna leave me," he said as he released his hold of her arms.

"No, baby! No!"

"Fuck! I know better. I knew it, but I was drinking with folks. Them and Man-Man's kept bitches wasn't loyal to nothing but money. And I let it get to my head."

"No, I wouldn't leave you. Tank was a trick of mine before I found out he was down with you, and I stopped fuckin' with him. Then out of nowhere he called me and followed me home. He said he really needed to talk to me. I let him in to hear what he had to say. That's when he started talking about me leaving with him. I told him no, and that's when he started acting crazy. I was scared, so I went along with it until I could get to my phone; but when I texted you, you, never hit me back."

When Scrap pulled her into his arms to hug her and apologize, she knew that he bought her story. But she was not going to let him get away with hitting on her this time.

# CHAPTER 9

Max explained to his PO that he had won a nice sum of money at the casino.

"I had them give me so many small bills so I wouldn't give them the whole nine Gs back. I got it rolled up like that because it's just a habit I got," he lied.

He could see from the expression on her face that she was not buying his story, and that was when he remembered the small sack of grams in his pocket.

"Fuck it, Munday! I'm tellin' ya the truth, and I can

see that you still don't believe me. So, fuck it! Go ahead and lock me up when I only got a little over a week to go before I'm off this shit. If that's what ya gonna do, It may as well be on some real shit," he yelled as he pulled the sack out of his pocket and tossed it at her feet. "That's paid for! Everything, but not the weed. The only reason I got so much weed is because it's the best buy. That's it! That's all! Now can I please get dressed before you lock me up?"

The way that Max put all his cards on the table and was not lying to her turned her on a bit. The fact that he was shirtless with his jeans hanging low on his waist only added to Ms. Munday already feeling for the thug. She had been daydreaming about Max almost since the first day he stepped foot in her office. To her Max had the pretty-boy swag on the outside but was all thug on the inside. She thought he was the kind of guy that looked good and could hold his own in a fight.

"No, you can't! I'm not that petty, Max," she said as she closed the space between them. "Thanks for being honest with me. I respect that." She dropped the ziplock bag on the floor beside her. "I'm going to have to take this, you know, and I need to pat you down to see what else you've been hiding from me."

"Do what ya want as long as it's not lockin' me back up."

With that she yanked down his jeans to expose his length. She then took hold of it. "I think I need to apologize for not believing you. Will you let me?"

Max was really thrown off by what was happening, but that did not stop the blood from rushing to his package in her warm hand.

"Do I got a choice?"

"No, you don't, 'cause mama got a yearning and in need of a fix, Mr. Dope Man," she said before she kissed and stroked him tenderly.

Max grabbed her by the throat with one hand and held her close to him with the other as he returned the kiss. On the inside he was nervous, but on the outside, he took control.

"Mmmmm, this is good, but not what I want," Ms. Munday said as she pulled away from his hold and then hiked up her skirt over her slim waist. "This is where I need your kiss."

Without another word, Max stepped out of the jeans around his ankles and slipped his fingers inside her. He exposed her black thong before he ripped it off. Her moan let him know she was enjoying his roughness. He noticed her light complexion was now flushed with lust. Max wanted and needed to please her to make sure she was on his team, so he dropped down and combined his tongue with the slow finger-fucking he was giving her.

Ms. Munday stood with one of her long legs over his strong shoulder. She was lost in the tongue lashing he was giving her. Within moments she was cumming and shaking, and freely giving him her juices. Max stopped just as her flow started. He then stood up, spun her around, and bent her over the sofa. He gave her nice round butt a few slaps and then slipped his hardness deep inside her wetness. He pounded her nice and hard while continuing to spank her. She let out loud cries of pleasure as he brought her daydreams to life.

When they were spent, Ms. Munday found the bathroom and went in to freshen up. Max's heart stopped when she walked out holding the gun that she found on the counter. He had forgotten it was in there and did not know how to explain it other than he needed to be safe.

"I guess I'm going to have to come back so we can address this later," she told him after placing the gun on the table and leaving all the drugs lying on the floor where they were.

She then let herself out of his apartment.

* * *

"I gotta get outta here. I'm going home," Champagne said as she refilled her drink from the bar in the corner of Scrap's office.

"Why, what's wrong? What, ya trippin'? 'Cause you was fuckin' that nigga?" he asked before closing the office door to block out the sound of them working Tank over and what he was about to do to her.

"I told you, I don't give a fuck about him. I just don't wanna be here around this no matter who it is," she answered before taking a sip of her drink.

Champagne was so scared that she could not

stop her hands from shaking.

"Come here!" he asked, which she did. "I don't want you to go. I need you here with me. You mine, and right now I need to be reminded of that." He pulled her to him in a tight hug, and then took her by the throat. "You're not dancing and turning tricks no fuckin' more." He applied pressure. "Yo' my bitch, and it makes me look bad, like I'm one of them weak-ass niggas."

Champagne was fighting to breathe when Murdah walked in. He was another high-ranking member of Murder Mob and a silent partner in Bonkerz.

"If you in here playin' hubby, who in there makin' sure I got my shit back?" he asked while standing behind Scrap and leaving the door ajar behind him.

Scrap let Champagne go.

"Fam, you didn't have to come here. I got this shit under control."

"Well Man-Man told me he was on it because you were having hoe problems. So, I did need to come to make sure yo' head is in the right place on this shit. I can go if you gonna pay me for the work that nigga ran off with."

"Murdah, I'm good. I don't know why he called you. You need to tell that lil' nigga to mind his and stay the fuck outta mine. He must think he's Badman's replacement or some shit."

"What happen to yo' folks?" Murdah asked, uninformed on the subject.

"Oh, the nigga didn't tell ya that, huh? Bad and Tommy got locked up outside in the parking lot. Champ said they got caught with a burner and some work. It just happened, so I ain't put nobody on it yet."

"Fam, that shit there is more important than whatever ya got going on in here," Murdah said as he took Champagne's drink out of her hand and finished it in one gulp. "Champ, go home! You don't need to be here. We got shit to do."

"But!"

"But nothing! He said go home!" Scrap cut her off.

Right then Man-Man walked out of the Adjustment Box. "Punk-ass nigga, I can beat yo' ass all night. This is fun for me. What about you?" he yelled at the badly beaten man. "What up, Unc? How long ya been here?" he asked Murdah.

"Long enough. What you got for me?"

"The nigga ain't saying shit. His bitch ass is just cryin' and shit."

"Scrap, get in there and make him talk," Murdah announced as he sat behind the desk. "Champ, why you still here?"

Champagne knew not to play with the cold-hearted gangster. There was nothing about the five-foot-nine, gold-toothed, and tat-faced man that said he liked to repeat himself. Champagne gathered up her things, gave Scrap a soulless kiss on the cheek, and made her way out the door. She told him to call her when he was free. She did not want Scrap to think she was leaving him, which was just what she was planning on doing—just not empty-handed.

The DJ and one of the bartenders were getting set up to open on the club floor. She told them she was not going to be in to work, and then walked out to her car. She drove around aimlessly. The only thing on her mind was how she was going to get revenge and escape, when Max popped into her head. She smiled to herself at her memory of their time together. Champagne made a U-turn and headed home.

When she arrived home, she saw a very attractive woman leaving Max's unit. Now Champagne knew that he was not her man and that

Max was still going to be sleeping with other women. She just expected it to be with someone who looked as good as herself.

The mental and physical abuse she went through at the club laced with seeing Ms. Munday leave Max's unit was a blow to her self-esteem. Instead of going to chill with Max, she kept walking and went straight to her place. She wanted to get herself together before she saw him, since she now knew that she had someone better than Kake to contend with.

# CHAPTER 10

It was back to the paper chase as always for the young thug Max. He had no idea what would happen next with his PO, and the gun was a distraction for him. When Ms. Munday did not return his calls or return to his place the night before like she said she would, Max started to worry and wonder if he should be on the run. He kind of felt that he was okay, but he needed to see his PO to be sure.

"I'ma just go in to see if the bitch is on some shit, or if she's in some type of way from how a nigga put it on her."

"Yo' ass a fool for that! I can't believe you fucked yo' PO. But, yeah, I do think you should go to see her. Come take me with you just in case I gotta come bail you outta jail."

"Kake, if she locks me up, I won't have a bail, 'cause it'll be a probation hold. But I'ma still come get you so you can take my car to my mom's crib if I get caught up," Max explained after dropping the blade on the table where he sat chopping up work. "Yeah, I'm on my way."

He ended the call with Kake, finished bagging the dope he had broken down, and put the rest up. When he opened his door to leave, Champagne was standing there just getting ready to knock.

"Whoa, where you in a hurry to?"

"Hey, I'm just making a run right fast. What up?" he asked before closing and locking the door behind him.

"Can I ride with you, or is this something you gotta do alone, 'cause I kinda wanna talk to you about something."

"Okay, then you can just drive me there, so I won't have to take my car," he told her as he sent a text to Kake telling her he got a ride to his PO's office and that he would call her later if he could.

"Okay, I need to run and get my bag. Where we going?" she asked, leading him back to her unit.

"I gotta go see my PO, and I don't wanna drive, just in case she's on one and put a hold on me."

"Man, what you do?"

"She found my banger when she made a surprise home visit the other day. She didn't take it, but she didn't come back to talk to me about it like she said she was." He made sure to leave out the part that they had sex before she found the gun. "And she ain't returning my calls," he further explained before stopping at Champagne's door.

"Was that the girl I saw leaving your place yesterday?" she asked when she unlocked the door.

Max wondered if she heard them.

"I guess. Where was you?"

"I was just pulling in when I saw her leaving. I thought she was one of your lil' bitches," Champagne answered, grabbing her purse and then locking up.

"Is that jealousy I hear? Tell me! Come on! It's okay! I won't judge!" he teased.

"Boy, please! She's your PO!" she lied, feeling relieved that she did not have her to compete with. "Max, I don't think you got shit to worry about, because if she was gonna do something, she would have done it right then and there. You must not have long to go."

"I only got like ten days left," he answered while getting into her car.

"Yeah! That bitch ain't trying to do no paperwork if you don't make her. I don't think you should go in there."

"Well fuck it! I'ma just wait her out then. But if I

get locked up, I'm gonna be lookin' for yo' ass to hold me down." He laughed.

"If things go rough, that's no problem. So now where can we go to get a drink while I run what I got in mind by you?"

"Go to Connie's on 40th and North," he instructed as she turned out of the alley.

* * *

Murdah instructed Scrap to leave the unconscious Tank tied up all night in the Adjustment Box. When Man-Man returned in the morning, Tank was ready to talk, but only with Scrap so he could bargain for his life. Scrap agreed and the three of them went for a ride to retrieve the drugs with which Tank had run off.

"Nigga! If ya lying to us, I'ma kill yo' whole fuckin' fam and make you watch me do it before I kill yo' dumb ass," Man-Man threatened Tank.

"I'm not, fam! You'll see. I fucked up, but I don't wanna die."

Once they reached Tank's safe house, he led them down to the basement to a deep freezer with a false bottom. The inside was filled with drugs and money, and there looked to be more than the sixteen kilos with which he had run off. Scrap knew this was all Tank had tucked away, but before he could press him to find out where he was hiding the rest, Man-Man shot Tank twice point-blank in the chest. Tank was dead before he hit the floor.

"What the fuck yo' dumb ass do that for?"

"Fuck that nigga! We got what we came for, right, fam, so fuck him. I told ya before that I ain't lettin' a muthafucka come back at me later."

"Nigga, this ain't all of it! He got more stashed somewhere else. This shit here was just to get us off his ass."

"Oh well, fam, ya should've told me that shit a long time ago!"

Scrap lost it and hit him twice hard in the face, and then snatched the gun out of his hand. "Fool-ass nigga! You don't run shit, I do! I should shoot yo' fool ass for this shit," he yelled at him before he hit him again. "Now get something to put this shit in, and then do something about this," he ordered as he began pulling out the contents of the freezer.

* * *

Inside Connie's restaurant, Max and Champagne sat at a table in the corner across from the DJ booth, so they could have some privacy and Max could keep his eye on the door.

"So, what's on yo' mind that ya needed a drink to talk about something?"

"What, you don't wanna be seen with me?"

"Don't care! I don't care where I'm seen with you. I was just making small talk since ya got me out here missing money and shit," Max answered, looking up from his phone and taking a gulp of his beer.

"Well, that's kinda what I wanna talk to you about."

For the first time she felt a bit nervous, but she

reminded herself that she was only a failure if she did not shoot her shot.

"The other day when you saw me with Tank, he asked me to go away with him." She paused to let Max comment if he wanted to, but she continued when he did not. "I told him I would think about it, but I'm not doing it. I just didn't want him to do something crazy to me."

"So, what, ya want me to handle this nigga or what?"

"Not him, just listen. Today when I went to the club to talk to Scrap, he jumped on me."

"Who jumped on you, Tank?"

"No, Scrap. He was talking about why I didn't tell him that Tank wanted me to leave with him."

"He put his hands on you 'cause a nigga told him that shit? That shit is cray!" Max said.

He then noticed the slight discoloration on her neck and jaw that she did a poor job of covering up with makeup.

"He didn't tell him he saw it in Tank's phone. The only reason Scrap ain't still whooping my ass is because I never told Tank I would go with him."

"Champ, I'm not gettin' in that shit. I don't see how it has anything to do with gettin' money."

"Listen, Max! Damn! Tank was bragging to me about having fifty bricks and a half a million."

"How do you know he wasn't just lying to get ya to go with him?"

"It's not the first time he talked about how much

money he was working with to me, and Scrap got him in a room in the basement of Bonkerz beating the shit outta him for stealing from them. He must not know where it is yet 'cause Scrap would've killed him over me."

"How the hell did he steal that much from him? Hell, if I'd hit a lick like that, I would've hit the highway ASAP and sent for yo' ass when I was good."

"Max, I can't take it anymore. Scrap's crazy! I'm nobody's punching bag," she admitted as she played with a water ring on the table from her beer. "I'm done with him and all this bullshit. I want to make him pay for all the times he put his hands on me. That's why I need your help. Max, I need you to help me rob him. I know every fucking thing about how he does shit, and I even know where his mine house is and everything."

Max could tell she was fighting back tears as she asked for his help.

"Champagne, I'm game if ya really wanna do this, but I need ya to think about it for a bit 'cause I'm not tryin' to end up in a nigga's basement. Tell me this. Did ya break up with him yet?"

"We wasn't ever together. He's just crazy claiming me. He told me I couldn't dance in his club anymore because it made him look weak. He's crazy! But I'ma play along with it until I can make my move. I don't know nothing about selling bricks or none of that shit, so you can have all that shit if you don't wanna fuck with me like for real."

"It sounds all good. Let's go back to the house and talk about this, 'cause I need to know all you do about how this nigga moves," Max said before finishing his beer.

# CHAPTER 11

A few hours later, Scrap called Champagne to his eastside home, which gave Max time to really put some thought into what he was thinking of getting into with her. He needed to know more about Tank and the others, so he went to have a talk with his buddy Slugga.

Over blunts and a game of Black Ops, Slugga listened to Max explain what Champagne wanted him to do.

"Man, them Murder Mob niggas is the truth! They're the real deal for real. On top of 'em having money, they're quick to pop off them burners," he warned Max while pausing the game and accepting the blunt from him.

"That's why I'm here hollerin' at you. I know I can do this shit. I just didn't know if the bitch really knew what she was talking about."

"From what ya told me so far, she knew a lot. Hell, if ya can find out where that nigga Tank stores his cars, you might get lucky there. He had me build stash boxes in his Camaro and Infiniti."

"I might know where one of 'em is at right now. Champ told me the Camaro was parked in back of Bonkerz. If it's still there, I'ma go get it. So, where's that spot at?"

"Whoa, my nigga! What do I get outta this? I like

money, too."

"Big homie, ya know I'ma bust whatever I find in there with ya. This here ain't got jack to do with ole girl," Max promised. "I hope there's enough in there, so I can cop that Yukon from yo' guy."

With that said, Slugga gave Max everything he needed to know about how to steal the car. Since he was the one that installed it, it would be easy for Max to get around the alarm. Max found the car right where Champagne told him it was. As soon as the opportunity presented itself, he was in the Camaro and gone in less than a minute. He drove it over to Kake's house, since she had a garage that no one used because no one in her house owned a car. She was at work, so Max did not have to deal with her asking questions, and he planned on having it stripped and gone before she knew it was ever there.

The first thing he did was locate the release lever to the secret chamber in the seat, which was right where Slugga said it would be. After Max opened it, he found a bag of cash, a gun, and drugs inside it. He emptied the stash box and then called his mechanic hype buddy, Fred, to come strip the car and get rid of the shell when he was done. Max gave Fred two grams to get started and promised him seven more when the job was done, since he was feeling generous because of his newfound wealth. Max then caught a cab back to Bonkerz where his car was parked to make sure his buddy had time. He stashed the loot in the trunk and went inside in search of Kake. He knew she would not turn down weed and a free ride home.

* * *

Latia Munday arrived at her West Allis apartment and needed to unwind from the last thirty hours or so. Moments after she made it in to work after her rendezvous with Max, she had to rush to the hospital with her grandmother. She had fallen and injured her hip, so Ms. Munday was unable to get back to Max for another round of mind-blowing sex. She kicked off her shoes, put on some relaxing music, and filled the tub with bubbles and hot water. When it was ready, Latia undressed as she walked to the kitchen for a cold bottle of Boones Farm. She then pulled out her battery-operated friend from the nightstand to have some fun in the bath.

In the tub she let her mind return to the morning of her affair with Max. Just the thought of it had her good and aroused. She dipped her fingers into her folds and around her clit until she began to cum. Ms. Munday wanted Max inside her, so she scooped up the big black dildo and then slowly pushed it inside her warmth. Her friend felt so much better than it did. She knew how it felt to have Max inside her. Ms. Munday went wild working the dildo in and out of her while doing her best to mimic Max's thrust. She went fast and then slow, and then soft and then hard. She continued until she felt spasms, which announced her powerful orgasm. She loudly screamed her lover's name as she gave it all up. Ms. Munday knew she was going to Max's place for the real thing after she checked on her grandmother in the morning. She hoped he did not think she was ignoring him.

* * *

When Champagne arrived at Scrap's home, she found him so wasted that he could hardly stand on his own. He reeked of alcohol, and his cocaine use was visible on his face as well as out on a serving dish sitting on the table. This was not the first time she had seen Scrap in his current condition, but it was the worst. It was a good thing for her that he passed out shortly after she got there. After she got him cleaned up and in bed, she tackled the mess around the house just in case the police made a house call for something the fool had done before she got there.

Champagne noticed that Scrap had his usual large amount of cash on him, but what was surprising to her was the large pillowcase of money he had lying about. She thought of taking it and running off right then and there, but she did not think she would get far. So she took a small stack of bills as payment for her being there and then went and stashed it in her car. She knew in his state, Scrap would not remember what he did with it. Champagne took a nice relaxing bath in his luxurious whirlpool tub, and then afterward she got in bed next to him and went to sleep.

She awoke to the smell of bacon and the song from *Frozen*. Champagne rolled out of Scrap's king-size bed and went to investigate, wearing nothing but her panties. In the dining room, she found two adorable young girls hard at work systemizing a large mess of cash on the table.

"Good morning," the two sang to her.

The younger one giggled at Champagne's nudeness.

"Are you looking for our daddy?" the older one asked after hushing her litter sister.

"Wow! Yes, and good morning to you two."

"Daddy, your girlfriend's looking for you!" the young girl yelled. "Daddy said not to be loud, Nana," her big sister scolded.

"He said that, so we wouldn't wake her up. She's right here now, so I didn't wake her up. She did it by herself."

Champagne smiled at the two sisters.

"Does he know y'all are in here playing with his money?"

"We're not playing with it. This is our job for the day."

"Yeah, daddy gave us each $10 and is taking us to the mall," the young girl explained excitedly.

"Champ, I was just about to wake you up so you can eat with us. These two Care Bears had me cook them breakfast, so I hope ya hungry," Scrap said when he walked out of the kitchen holding two plates of food for the girls.

"Don't give them that until they wash their hands after messing with that money," Champagne suggested.

"Y'all do as she says, and then come eat. You can finish up when ya done eating."

The sisters ran off to the bathroom to wash their hands.

"So, you finally let me meet your daughters."

"I didn't plan on it. I didn't know they were coming. Some shit came up with my BM, so I got them for a few hours," he answered for their plates of food. "As much as I love to see you like this, go put something on."

"Oh shit! My bad. It's a habit," Champagne apologized before she then turned to go do as he said.

"Champ, thanks for coming over and cleaning

up. I was so chopped that I don't remember calling you."

She did not believe that Scrap did not remember calling her, but she went along with it, knowing she had been tested.

"So, what's this money out like this for, if ya don't mind me asking?" she questioned while standing in front of the table where it was piled.

The girls raced out of the bathroom.

"Y'all can go watch television in the front and eat today, but please don't get food on my couch," he told them. "Let's go back in the kitchen where they can't hear us."

She followed him back into the kitchen, where he explained the events around the money.

"So, what happened to Tank?"

She knew she had messed up as soon as the words left her lips.

"Don't ask me shit like that. Fuck him!" he said as he clenched his fist. "Man-Man's dumb ass was on some shit last night. The nigga set the house on fire after we ransacked it while lookin' for the rest of the money and shit that Tank stole."

Champagne's heart hurt a little because she knew they killed Tank. She started to wonder if the real reason she was called over to his house was to make sure she did not talk.

"Well, I need some money so me and the girls can go to the mall like you promised them, and I messed up my nails fuckin' with you last night." She then led him back into the dining room. "We don't need to be here for this; and since I work in the club, I know where this money has been. I don't want them cuties touching it like that."

Strap knew she was right, so he picked up a stack of bills and then walked over to the currency counter and inserted the stack.

"How much is this shopping spree gonna cost me?"

"Press start and I'll tell you how I feel about the number it stops on," she answered, taking his hand and placing it between her warm thighs. "You know you standing here with all this money makes me wanna cum."

She helped him press the button with her free hand as she ran her tongue along his ear.

# CHAPTER 12

The total amount of cash Max found in the Camaro was $33,000. As promised he broke off Slugga a nice chunk of it after he deducted the $8,000 for the GMC Yukon on which he had his eye. Max gave Slugga $12,000 as his cut and for him to install the new audio and video system in the truck.

"Max, you know them rims will go right on here, don't you?" Slugga said, noticing how he was looking at the rims from the Camaro that were stacked in the yard. "Yeah, they're universal. If you take off the backgrounds, it'll be hard for a nigga to tell that they came off the ‘Maro,” he explained, hoping to encourage Max.

“That’s what I’m talkin’ about! Let’s slap ‘em bitches on. I was just thinkin’ about how good they would look on the truck. They match the interior and the tints, so I’m good.”

“The only thing I would change if I was you is the tires. Them slims ride like crap on a truck. If I call my guys up at Pops and Sons, they can swap ’em out for you right fast, and maybe give you a discount for the old ones since they’re in good shape.”

“Let’s do it!”

An hour later they were returning from the tire shop, when Max noticed the familiar-looking Acadia parked in Champagne’s parking spot.

"Man, I think that's my PO's truck," he informed Slugga before he nervously pulled right beside it so he could get a good look inside.

"Damn, my nigga. That's yo' PO? I see why you hit that. I thought you were jackin' about how fine she was, but damn!"

Max got out of the truck, walked over, and tapped on the window of the Acadia, breaking Ms. Munday's attention from her iPad.

"So, you don't answer my calls or nothing and then just pop up at my crib? I believe that's an abuse of your rights or some shit."

"No, it's not!" She smiled before she put her window back up and got out.

"As long as you're on paper, I can drop in any

time I want for a home visit."

"So that's what this is? What, ya ready to let me know what ya gonna do about the gun?"

"I forgot about that, but thanks for the reminder." She smiled. "No, this visit is more personal. I feel we need to talk about the last time I was here, so we will have a clear understanding of things."

"Okay, well let me get rid of my guy, and then we can go inside and talk."

"Tell him I like his truck and ask him if it's okay for me to look inside."

"It's mine! I just got it last night. I was going to call you first thing Monday and tell you about it," he lied.

"In that case, get rid of him and let's go for a ride.

I've never ridden in a tricked-out car before," she excitedly admitted before she then walked around the Yukon and peeped through the windows at the five monitors and four 14-inch subwoofers that took up the whole trunk space.

"I heard her, my nigga, so go handle yo' business. Hit me when you can," Slugga said before he gave him dap, got into the Ford Five Hundred that he bought with his cut of the money, and raced off.

"So, where do you wanna ride to, Ms. Munday?"

"Call me Tia. I think after what we did the last time I was here, it gives you the right to use my first name, unless you just like the sound of it," she giggled.

"Okay, Tia! Where we going?"

“I don’t care! Let’s just ride and talk. Can you turn on the television for me?” she asked as she climbed in the passenger seat.

Max put on a Source R&B DVD for her and then turned down the subs, so they could talk as he cruised the city. He felt like a real boss sitting high in his truck with a bad bitch and a pocketful of cash. What topped off his feeling was knowing that he had almost half a kilo back at the house from the stash box. Max was really feeling himself. He listened as Tia explained why she did not return his calls, and she admitted that she could not stop thinking of that morning with him. Max admitted the same to her. He wanted to know if he really had a chance to be with her again.

"I was wondering if we could do it again soon but take our time next time." She blushed at her suggestion.

"It's gonna be busy for me tonight, so I won't be able to give ya all my attention at my place." He could see the disappointment in her eyes. "But we're together now, sooooo?"

"So, let me find out if you can make me cum as fast as you did before," she challenged him. "We can get a room. My treat since my place is off limits for now."

"Off limits? Why, 'cause yo' nigga there?" he questioned as he drove through the east side of town weaving through the side streets.

"No, I don't have one of those. I just don't take

men home who I'm unsure want to stick around."

"I think you should help me break in my truck before we have a discussion about me sticking around or not. Hell, right now that's all up to you!"

"You can relax, Max. I don't plan on sending you back to HOC. I'm not that way."

"That's good to know. Now take off yo' panties," he ordered her while never taking his eyes off the road.

Letoya Luckett's music video was playing in the background. She was rapping something about being the love doctor. Even though the sun was out, they were behind heavily tinted windows.

"You're not worried about me cumming on your seat?" she asked, already deciding she would do it.

"That's the purpose for me tellin' you to take off yo' clothes. Now stop stallin' and get to it!"

He smiled and then turned up the powerful subwoofers just enough for them to vibrate the seats. Max's authoritativeness was turning her on more than just being alone in the truck with him. Tia kicked off her white casual leather Nikes and then wiggled out of her tight Seven jeans.

"Oops! I forgot to put undies on today," she giggled.

"That's even better!" He took a quick glance at her shapely thighs. "Open yo' legs so I can see that smile." She did, and Max wet his lips as they pulled up to a stop sign. "Play with it for me. I wanna see ya make yo'self cum."

"You gonna kill us watching me while you're driving," she told him, feeling the excitement of it all rushing through her.

"I got this. You just do what I say, or I can just take you back to yo' ride and get someone else to help me break in my truck."

Tia faked a shocked expression as her hand dove down between her thighs. She let her fingers dance with her clit, just like they had done many times in the past. Max found a secluded place to park and then took over what she was doing to herself as he kissed and teased her like the seasoned lover he was.

She moved her seat all the way back with one hand and undid his pants with the other. Then she leaned over and took him in her hand.

"You're so hard. Sit back and let me do something about it," she asked while stroking him as he adjusted his seat for her.

Tia bent down in his lap and licked the head of his hardness. She then skillfully took all of him in her mouth. She kept alternating between deep-throating and licking his length until she could taste his pre-cum.

"I want you in me, Max. I need you in me."

"Say no mo'!"

He climbed over the gearshift and between her wide-open legs. Tia braced one foot on the dash and the other leg over his shoulder as he long-stroked her nice and hard until they came almost at once.

When they looked up, they caught an elderly white man with a little brown dog watching them with the biggest grin on his face. In the heat of the moment, they forgot about the windshield not being tinted.

"Now that you've fucked me good, you gotta feed me, Max," she told him, leaning back into her seat with a satisfied smile on her face.

"Yeah, okay, but I'm not done with you yet," he promised her before he tapped the horn and drove past the man and his dog.

When they made it back to Max's after picking up takeout from Olive Garden, all their plans were placed on hold due to the line of hypes waiting on him to get there. This was the first time Ms. Munday had ever truly witnessed this side of any man or woman she had on supervision. She found out that it was fast money but not easy money. She admired the way Max handled all the dope heads.

"You can go if ya want. I can tell right now that it's gonna be a busy night," he told her after he made it back inside from emptying out his second two-hundred-gram sack since they made it back to his place.

"Oh no, buddy. You're not getting rid of me. This is kinda fun and educational for me," she answered excitedly. "What can I do to help out? Oooh, can you teach me how to whip it?" Tia asked as she pulled her hair back in a braid and let it fall across her shoulder.

# CHAPTER 13

Champagne took a chance and went into work because Lil Boosie was in town and was rumored to stop at Bonkerz. She was not about to miss a chance to meet the rap star; besides, she already missed the excitement of being onstage.

At the club she dressed in a pair of red and white studded chaps with matching bra and panties. She added a pair of high clear wedges with colorful flashing lights in them. Lil Boosie jumped on the runway stage and performed his hit song "Ain't Comin Home Tonight."

*I ain't comin' home tonight, I know it ain't right*

*I know it ain't right,*

*But I ain't comin' home tonight.*

*I know it ain't right, I know it ain't right.*

*But I ain't comin' home tonight,*

*'Cause tonight I'm on flight,*

*Tonight, I'm on flight.*

The first face Champagne saw when she exploded through the door was Scrap. But she knew he would not make a scene with the artist onstage, so she stayed focused on putting on the best show of her life for Lil Boosie and the many patrons that surrounded the stage to see them.

## CASH IN CASH OUT

*Me and my girl just had a fight.*

*I gotta get away.*

*Look like I ain't comin' home for a couple days,*

*I hit the plane.*

*Chill!*

*Put on my shades.*

*On da plane can't shhhh.*

*Now I'm in a daze.*

*A high kosher,*

*You remember dem Lil Boosie days*

*I broke ya virgin at 15,*

*Now you feel played*

*By da way.*

*Why dem bruises on yo' fuckin' face?*

*She said my man still bringin' up that Boosie*

*case.*

*What's yo' destination?*

*Florida.*

*Dat's where I'm goin', too.*

*I'm at da same hotel you at*

*Room 102.*

*And you can come to my room,*

*But she said no.*

*She said no, you can come to mines.*

*I got a surprise.*

*I walked up into da room*

*And smelled was the best.*

*She had on a lil' red dress.*

*I ain't comin' home tonight.*

As he rapped, Champagne scaled the pole all the way to the top and then let herself fall, spinning hands free and using only her legs to stop about a foot from the floor. She did the first part of her set on the pole mostly because she was trying to stay as far away from Scrap as she could, so he would not make her get off the stage. But by the time Lil Boosie went into his second song, she joined the rest of the dancers onstage. As the crowd made it rain dollars for her, she made her ass clap in between dropping it like it was hot for them.

* * *

Since it was that time of the month for Kake, she worked as a server at the club for the night and only did hands-free wall dances here and there. As Kake was on her way to deliver drinks, she heard a girl in one of the VIP rooms screaming for help. Kake quickly burst into the room and repeatedly cracked the big man across his back and shoulders with the champagne bottle from her tray. The girl was able to push him off of her, which caused him to stumble and for Kake to get in a good whack. She hit him hard in the head, dropping him just as the bouncers rushed into the room. They beat and kicked the drunk would-be rapist all the way out of the club and into the cuffs of an awaiting police officer who just happened to be in the area. Then it was back to business as usual in the club. The incident did not stop or slow down anything that was going on, on the other side of Bonkerz.

* * *

Scrap had both Kake and the tall, sexy, and scantily dressed girl at the center of the disturbance in the club escorted down to his office.

"I was only doing my job when I heard her screaming for help. When I went in to see what was going on, that muthafucka was all over her and trying to rape her. I was only lookin' out for my girl. Please don't fire me, Scrap. I need my job," Kake pleaded while standing in front of the other girl.

"Hey, hey! Ms. Kake, you good. This is not about your job. It's about hers," he said as he pointed to the other girl. "Who the hell are you, and who told you that you can work in my club? Now before you lie to me, I need you to know that I've had a hand in hiring everyone in this club."

"I don't work here. I'm Champ's friend, Playthang. She told me to come in for immature night."

Scrap cut her off.

"It's not immature night, so try again!"

Playthang stepped closer.

"I know. I was here on Wednesday, but I lost my nerve and went home. I came in tonight to see Boosie, and when I saw Champagne on the stage, I just wanted to prove to myself that I could do it."

"So, Ms. Kake, you don't know her?"

She shook her head no.

"Okay, go back to work, and you're paying for that bottle you wasted. And when you get up there, send Champ down here," he ordered Kake before he turned and focused back on Playthang. "Well, bitch, since you wanna prove yo'self so bad, show me what you workin' with," he told her as he took his seat behind his desk.

When Kake walked out, Champagne was already standing there.

"Good, he wants to see you. Let me know what he's on later."

Champagne agreed before she entered the office and then closed and locked the door behind her.

"Oooh, girl, are you alright?" Champagne asked once she saw the bruises on her friend's face.

"Yeah, I'm good. I didn't mean to get you in no

mess," Playthang whispered as they hugged.

"Girl, I'm good. I got this." Champagne held her hand and then addressed Scrap. "Bae, don't be mad at her. I told her to come to the club to try out. I meant to talk to you about her, but there's been so much going on that I forgot."

"I know all that already, Champ, but friend or not, I'ma need to see what this bitch is workin' with and if she can dance before she can step foot on my stage. You know this."

"See, that's what I wanna talk to ya about. Playthang is!"

"No, Champ, I should be the one to tell him," Playthang interrupted. "Boss man, I'm not all what you see yet. That's why I wanna work in the club, so

I can finish making my outside match my insides."

"So, what, you a man?" he asked in surprise. "You shittin' me, right?"

"No, I'm so serious. Here, see for yo'self," Playthang said as she slowly started to remove her clothes.

Champagne walked behind the desk and sat in Scrap's lap, just in case her suspicion of him was off.

"Whoa, girl, ya know this is my favorite part. Give us the whole show," she encouraged her with a smile as she felt Scrap's hard-on growing against her butt.

"Fuck, this shit is crazy! Turn around so I can have another good look at you," Scrap told Playthang after tightening his hold on Champagne.

Playthang did as she was told and showed off

her five-foot-ten body. Scrap was turned on. He took in her tall and slim waist, wide mouth, bright gray eyes, black-and-blond curls that fell down her back, and nice C-cup tits.

"So, this is the reason that nigga was in there whoopin' on yo' ass, ain't it?"

"No, that fool knew what he was getting. I don't play with my life like that. That muthafucker wanted to fuck me, and I know that you don't play that in the club. So, I said no, and he got rough with me," Playthang explained.

"She hot, ain't she?" Champagne asked as she slowly ground her ass in his lap. "Let's take her home to play, please?"

"Champs, I ain't doin' no shit like that. I ain't gay."

"I know, bae. She's not either. And don't nobody gotta know but the three of us. Come on, do it for me."

Champagne climbed out of his lap, pushed his chair back, and then dropped down between his legs and pulled out his hardness through his zipper.

"Playthang, come here and help me with this big boy."

"Champ, what the fuck did I just tell you?"

"I heard you, but I'm not tryin' to hear that shit."

She took his hand and placed it on Playthang's nice firm implants.

When he did not fight or pull away, Playthang took her place down on her knees next to her friend. Then together they licked, kissed, and sucked him until he gave them what they were working for. He held Playthang's head in place, and she happily swallowed every last drop of Scrap's release while unknowingly confirming for Champagne what she had thought about Scrap to be true.

# CHAPTER 14

Eventually they got some more free time and went to bed, but Tia was still too excited to get in a good rest. She tossed and turned until the morning light peeked in through her bedroom window. After Max took a break from answering his hustle bell, he took her out to Denny's to get a quick bite to eat. They got the meal to go because Tia asked him to take her home, so she could get a change of clothes and a few other things she needed to spend the weekend with him.

When they got to her house, Max was so

exhausted that he fell asleep on her loveseat by the time she had her overnight bag packed. Since Tia had already broken her rule about bringing men to her place with whom she was not serious, she decided to let him stay, knowing he needed the rest. Tia could imagine doing what she had witnessed Max do every day and still be sane. She was able to wake him up long enough to undress him and get him into her bed before she took a shower and climbed in with him.

That was hours ago, and now Tia was awake and aroused by the thought of him out cold and lying next to her. Feeling frisky, she started off kissing and half sucking on his shoulder while she slipped her hand between her warm thighs. That was when she got the idea to see how far she could get before Max woke up and caught her. She flipped the covers back, so she could have full admittance to the sexy thug. Then she went to work nibbling her way down his body, letting her tongue taste and tease his nice hard abs before moving on. Without using her hands, she found his semi-hard length and sucked it between her soft lips and then inside her mouth.

Her fingers went back to work on her clit as she gave him the best head she had ever given in her twenty-seven years. Tia was so caught up in the pleasure she was giving herself that she did not notice that Max had woken up until he pulled her up and rolled on top of her. His hardness easily found its way inside her wetness, and he did not stop until he was balls deep. He stayed there while he kissed and nibbled on her neck, collarbone, and then nipples. He then rolled his hips and made his thickness stretch and open up her tight, wet box more and more. Tia came hard just as Max filled her with his warm release.

A moment later as they lay trying to catch their breath, her phone started ringing the tone set for her grandmother. The call was from her grandmother's personal care worker who informed Tia that her Grandma Munday had to be rushed to the hospital again. They got up and rushed out the door. Max offered to take her straight to the hospital, but Tia insisted on him taking her to her truck, so she could go alone. Once he got back to his place, and Tia was off dealing with her family issue, he made up his mind to help Champagne bamboozle her guy.

He sat in his truck looking at his car and thinking of how far he had come in the short time since he got out of HOC. That was when he sent the text to Champagne: “Come see me as soon as you can if you still wanna party yo’ guy.”

* * *

After the club, Scrap was a no-show at the hotel. He gave Champagne an excuse about having to pick up his daughters in the morning. She knew it was a lie because he sent a text instead of calling. Since the room was paid for, Champagne and Playthang turned the remainder of the night into a slumber party with just the two of them. They took long hot showers, bought junk food from the vending machines on the hotel floor, and rented two movies.

Champagne listened to her friend tell her about growing up and feeling like she was living someone else's life.

"So, you've never been with a girl?" Champ asked, after pausing the second movie, *War Horse*, to give Playthang her full attention.

"No, not unless you count the kissing game I used to play with my step-sister when I was like ten," she chuckled. "Have you ever did it with a girl?"

"Girl, yeah!" Champagne admitted after she repositioned herself on the full-size bed. "I ain't ever been with a girl like you, though," she said with a smile. "I'm bi, but I like men more. A dildo just don't taste the same!"

"Oooh, you so right! A bitch gotta have something that can quench her thirst at the end."

They laughed.

"Sooooo, Play, do ya wanna know how it feels to be with one?" Champagne asked as she reached over and rubbed the bulge in Playthang's boy shorts.

"I don't know," she answered self-consciously.

"That's not the answer I'm feeling right now."

"You want me to do it with you?"

"Yeah, I'm right here. Shit! It'll be the best of both worlds for me, and I got my friend in my bag so you won't feel left out."

"Fuck it! Why not!" Playthang conceded as she got turned on by Champagne fondling her.

"Okay, now stand up and take yo' top off so I can see what ya workin' with," she said in her best Scrap impression. "Just leave yo' briefs on for now. I don't wanna spoil my surprise."

Playthang peeled away from her and did as she was told, and then performed a little striptease for her friend. Champagne sat back on the bed and watched Playthang gyrate her nice-sized erection in front of her face. Champagne got on her knees in the bed and softly kissed her. Playthang then ran her fingers through the seductress, deepening their osculation.

"Play, we don't gotta rush. We got until checkout, and it's just the two of us," Champagne reminded her.

Champagne started sucking and kissing Playthang's neck, which sent light shivers through her body. Just feeling Playthang's tremors made her hotter. She then removed her bra.

"Touch me the way I know you've touched these," she ordered while pulling her onto the bed with her.

Playthang used her wide mouth and long tongue to tease and tickle Champagne's hard nipples in a way that made her back arch and made her purr. That was when Champagne ventured by sucking on her friend's soft implants while sliding her hand inside her briefs.

"Take these off for me?"

Playthang removed them and let her length

spring free.

"So ya do like me?" Champagne said while wetting her lips.

Playthang blushed.

"Champ, you're the only girl that's ever made it salute."

"In that case, lay down so I can see what's up."

"Oooh, can we do it 69? I've always wanted to try it that way."

"Girl, this is our time. We can do whatever ya want and however ya want, but you can't be shy with that tongue when ya get down there," she told her before she pushed her down on the bed and got on top of her tall, creamy body.

Playthang went right to work with her long fingers

dipping inside Champagne's hot spot. Champagne was so wet that she needed Playthang's thick white length inside her wetness instead of in her mouth. Champagne could tell that Playthang was enjoying the taste of her cum by the way she parted her lips with her fingers and then sucked and flicked her button with her tongue. It felt so good to her that she lost her fluctuation with the hardness between her lips. So, she rolled away from Playthang's hungry mouth and straddled her hard-on backward. As soon as it entered her, she was cumming, and soon Playthang was bucking her hips and sending her thickness deeper and harder into her.

Both of them were soon moaning loudly, and Champagne came harder as Playthang released her juice deep inside her. That's when Champagne heard the ringtone play that she set for Max on her phone. She got up and retrieved her phone, already knowing it was a text from how short the song was.

"Bitch, I think you turned me gay!" Playthang told her smiling from ear to ear.

"And I ain't done with ya yet," Champagne promised as she responded to the text.

# CHAPTER 15

Max played it safe and rented a maroon Chrysler Pacifica, not knowing how much Scrap knew about him—if he knew anything at all. He made sure the windows were tinted just enough to still blend in with other vehicles that commonly flew through the upper-middle-class neighborhood. Champagne had given him the address and layout of the home as best she could. Now Max sat parked up the block from the house for almost two hours, peeping out the movements surrounding his target.

He was dressed in dark gray Dickie cargo pants

and a Milwaukee Brewers T-shirt with matching baseball cap to help the thug blend in the area nicely. When the street lamps popped on, Max moved closer to the house but not right in front, so he would not have anything in the way when he made his getaway. As casually as he could, he walked up to the house and found Scrap's Cadillac CTS parked at the back of the driveway, but Max knew that he was at the club from the text he had gotten from his accomplice a half hour ago, so he continued on.

Max looked through a window to be sure the house was empty, and then he pulled a short crowbar from his pants and jammed it in between the door lock. The lock easily gave way, which he was a bit surprised about, knowing what should be inside the house. He crept inside, and the first thing he noticed was the flashing light on the alarm pad, something that Champagne forgot to tell him about. He quickly rushed through the house, banking on a slow response time from the police.

Max found the bedroom where he was told Scrap kept the goods. He did not waste time on the lock; he just kicked open the door. Inside he found two large safes that he knew he would not be able to move or get into on his own. With nothing else to do and pressed for time, Max grabbed a metal lockbox from the table in the room and fled from the house. As soon as Max made it behind the wheel of his vehicle, a squad car raced onto the block with its lights and siren blasting. He ducked down in the seat just in time for the cop to speed by him. Then he calmly drove away from the scene.

Once safely back on his side of town, Max parked the Pacifica two blocks up from his place and walked home with the lockbox hidden in a Walmart shopping bag.

Now safely inside his unit, he sent a text to Champagne that read: “Back early from my trip. Could not get in without my key. Come see me for some fun when you can.”

Then he went to work on opening the box by using a hammer and screwdriver. After about five minutes of beating on the box, the lock popped open. Max’s hard work was rewarded with rows of neatly stacked cash and a written note with the total amount on it.

Max contemplated keeping it all for himself since Champagne did not tell him about the alarm. But then he decided to be straight with her since she was so close to Scrap, and he might mention to his girl what he was missing. Instead, he pressed play on his radio and filled the room with the sounds of Gucci Mane's hit "Hood Up," and sat down to count the loot as he rapped along. When he finished, it totaled out to the same $50,000 that was written on the note. Content with his take, he opened up shop for the night.

# CHAPTER 16

The following morning, Champagne was knocking on Max's door. Even though he knew it was her, he still checked to be sure before he opened the door. The first thing she noticed were the neat stacks of money. She could tell it was from the house by the way it was banded together.

"What happened? I thought you couldn't get it?" she asked while walking over to the table to get a closer look.

"I couldn't! That's a concellation prize because somebody didn't tell me about the fuckin' alarm. So, a nigga had to get in and out that bitch fast," he answered as he pulled on a shirt." I grabbed a lockbox off the table on the way out. But even if that alarm wasn't on, I still couldn't get them big-ass safes outta there by myself."

"Damn, how big are they?"

"Shit, about the size of the icebox. I thought ya said you been in that room?" Max asked, drinking a Red Bull for breakfast.

"Max, it's too early to be drinking that. You need to eat something first."

"Is you offering to cook? If not, then this and a blunt is how I'ma start my day off."

"No but give me my cut of this and I'll buy?" she answered while patting the money.

"Okay, that'll work. That's yours—the whole twenty racks—and I'm feeling steak, eggs, and pancakes to start with."

Champagne was impressed that he gave her so much without her knowing how much he had gotten.

"That's cool. We going to George Webb's on the south side, so we can talk in peace. You do know what happened with the alarm is a good thing, right?" she told him as she put the money in the waistline of her jeans because they were too tight for her to put it in her pockets.

"Why ya say that?" he asked, putting on his Nike Air Max 95s. "And, Champ, you can leave that here until we get back. I wouldn't rob you for it when I just gave it to ya."

"I know, but I gotta get my purse anyway." She opened the door and saw that the rain had really started coming down since she came in. "Damn, I'ma get fuckin' soaked running up there and back."

"Here, take my coat!" Max handed her a blue leather Pelle coat. "What do you need in yo' purse anyway? You got yo' phone and your keys. Fuck it and get that shit when we get back. I'm hungry as a muthafucka now that you brought it up," Max told her while pulling on a gray Pelle and the baseball cap he wore to Scrap's house the night before.

Champagne agreed to go without her purse, but she stuffed her money in the pockets of the big coat, and then they made a mad dash to the Yukon.

"When did you get this?" she asked while quickly

getting inside.

"I had it for a minute. It was in the shop?" he lied, wondering if she recognized the rims.

"Oh, I thought you had one of yo' guys over here when I came home," she told him, checking out the inside and liking the leather and rosewood.

"You didn't finish telling me why ya think we can still pull that lick off," he reminded her as they pulled away from the house.

"Oh yeah! Before I left, Scrap told me that he had a break-in at the house, so he would be busy moving his stuff around until the investigation was done. Max, you didn't leave no fingerprints, did you?"

"No, it's good! I don't think that's the kinda investigation the nigga's talking about," he said as he made a left down Walnut Avenue. "But do ya know where he's gonna move it to is the question?"

"Knowing that nigga the way I do, he's gonna take it to his office at Bonkerz. Scrap got a taste of OCD, so he's gonna count it. I mean he gonna count every last dime of it all over. I'm surprised he told me anything was missing."

"Hold up! So now ya want me to hit the club where all his niggas be? That shit is crazy!"

He shook his head and then took off his cap and tossed it on the back seat.

"Yeah, Max, the shit is easier than you think. He has trust issues, so I know he ain't gonna tell too many it's there, and he got a personal door that leads from the parking lot right in his office. I know for sure it don't got an outside alarm on it because he don't want the police down there at all. He got it hooked up, so it only alerts him down in his office and on his cell," Champagne explained as Max was entering the south side on 16th Street.

Max got quiet as he considered what she was proposing.

"Okay, Champ, ya know if this don't go right, it can fall back on you. I think we need somebody else to throw the heat on. I'm not trying to get thrown under the bus if he gets on yo' ass. How much do you think it is in them bad boys anyway?"

"I couldn't tell you but give me some time and a bitch will have an exact number for you if you need it. And as far as getting somebody to throw under the bus, I got that covered, but it's gonna cost us five Gs a piece to make it happen."

"Damn, I can have the nigga killed for less than that," he complained, turning into the parking lot of the diner.

"Yeah, but it's worth it. Just look at what you got out of a little box and shit. Either way we still fifteen stacks to the good, so it's win-win."

"Okay, I'll give it to you when we get back to the house," he gave in to her suggestion before he then got out of the truck and followed his nose to the smell of the food.

* * *

Later that day after a good nap, Champagne got up and texted Playthang to come over, so they could talk. She then called Scrap to see how things were going with him.

"Hey, bae, what you doing?"

"Hell, still moving this stuff to the office. Ya know I don't like everybody in my business, so it's just me and Man-Man doing all this shit. I heard water. Where you at?"

"I'm at home, baby. I just woke up and called you right away," she answered, knowing how he got when his jealousy kicked up. She decided to get off the phone just to tease that emotion. "Hey, baby, just call me when you're done so I can bring you something to eat and chill with you before things get too poppin' in the club."

"Champagne, ya must think I forgot that I told yo'

ass you couldn't work in the club no mo'?"

"No, I know you ain't forgot, but I like to dance 'cause it keeps me in shape. Nigga, ya know as soon as a bitch gets fat, you're gonna drop my ass for the next bitch and I'ma have to catch a case."

"On who?" he laughed. "You better be talkin' about the bitch 'cause I'll whoop that ass if ya run up on me about anything I do."

Scrap continued to laugh, but she did not find it funny because of all the times he had put his hands on her out of anger.

"Let me get off this line so I can get this shit done. And I don't give a fuck what ya bring me to eat; just make it double. I ain't ate shit since this happened."

"Okay, I'll see you when I get there," she told him

before she ended the call.

She walked into the bedroom to find something to dress in for the day. By the time she settled on a pair of white Guess jeans, a fitted Couture rayon shirt, cream suede Prada ankle boots, and a raw cotton biker jacket to complete the ensemble, Playthang was at her door.

"Girl, didn't you say you needed another $10,000 to give the doctor for yo' surgery?" she asked, walking around in only bra and panties as she finished her hair before she dressed.

"Yeah, I'm hoping to get the money up by my birthday, but it's not looking good for me right now. Why you ask?" Playthang asked, thinking about the sex she had with Champagne the last time they were alone like this.

"I asked 'cause I got five Gs for you. The catch is I need you to help me with a little something that's very important," she answered as she wiggled into her jeans.

"Champagne, you know I got you on whatever you need. You don't gotta pay me. Just tell me what you need that's so important."

"I'm tryin' to get the fuck away from Scrap. I'm sick of his bullshit. I know he's fuckin' one of them punk-ass bitches at Bonkerz. I just don't know who it is yet."

"So, what, you need me to pick them hoes' brains and see who I come up with for you?" she asked while standing up from her seat on the bed.

"No, it won't work 'cause everybody knows you're my ace. I need you to help me set him up so I can catch him in the act," Champagne said, stopping in front of her. "Play, I know the nigga like you. Scrap talks that tough shit, but he got a little sugar in his tank. If you do this for me, I can milk him for some cash—enough so we can both get what we want and still bounce on his fool ass in the end. I'm giving you this money because I want to help you become who you are, not for you doing this. I just said it wrong at first," Champagne explained, giving her the $5,000 she swindled out of Max, so she could keep hers all to herself.

# CHAPTER 17

The office looked like Scrap had robbed a bank. He had money stacked on almost every surface. Playthang could not believe her eyes when she walked in with Champagne to bring him something to eat after their little shopping trip. Champagne brought him all of his favorite dishes from Wong's Wok, including egg rolls, shrimp fried rice, and pepper beef with gravy.

They found Scrap busy ironing money, so it would fit smoothly into the two currency counters that sat side by side on the mini bar in the corner of the room.

"Scrap, here, take a break and eat. You look like shit. Have you been doing this since I called you?" Champagne questioned, moving a few things around to make space on the desk before she set down the hot food.

"No, I was just getting everything moved over here, and then I started my count," he replied before he glanced at Playthang and checked out her full cleavage in her snug, low-cut Barbie Doll tee. "Why you bring her down here with me doing this?"

"I didn't know. She's been with me all morning. Ya know I would not have brought her down here had I known it was like this."

"You don't gotta worry about me saying shit

about this here. Like I told you before, I love my life. I mean, damn! Like how much money is this anyway, and why are you still working yourself when you got all of this?" Playthang asked, not hiding her amazement.

"Bitch! I gotta worry about everybody, but it's good to know that ya know what will happen to you about this!" he warned. "But how ya start is how ya finish. I'm still in this because I ain't finished yet," Scrap bragged.

"I can help you if you want me to."

"Yeah, baby. Let her help you. I got a doctor's appointment to go to in a few, and she'll just be sitting around waiting for me to get done. If you let her help you, she won't be bored," Champagne proposed while taking his hand and leading him behind the desk.

"Yeah, but I can't trust no muthafucka's count but my own with this. Ya should know that already as long as you been around me," he told her while sitting down and opening up the carton of beef and gravy.

"Trust and believe I do know." She snatched the hot meat off his fork and ate it, just as he was about to put it in his mouth.

"Really! That's how ya do me, Champ?" He shook his head and laughed. "I bet you didn't get yo'self nothing, did you?"

"Well, I can do the ironing and get it all nice and flat for you, and after I'm finished, I can run it through your money thingy. I can put the bands on it. Oh, and just so you know, I'm not a muthafucka," Playthang offered secretly while winking at her friend.

He thought about being alone with her for a moment before he answered.

"Okay, you can do that, but if you try to steal from me or say anything about this, it's not gonna end well for you. I don't play about my money, and especially about this money here," Scrap warned her before he forked some food into his mouth. "You can start with that over there where I was."

"Alright then, I'm gonna take off so I won't be late. My appointment might be a couple hours depending on how many people he got in front of me since I'm a call-in," Champagne lied.

"Hey, Champ. Here! Take my keys and lock the door to the club and use the other door to leave. As a matter of fact, take my spare so you can get back in when you return. Just call me so ya won't get shot when ya come in."

Champagne did what Scrap asked her to do and then left him alone with Playthang. Her plan to get him alone with Playthang so she could seduce him went easier than she imagined. When Scrap gave her the key to his personal entrance, it made things a whole lot easier for Max to do what they talked about. She headed straight to a locksmith that she knew she could pay to ignore the "do not duplicate" warning on the key.

* * *

Max received a text from Tia informing him that her grandmother had passed away from heart failure and that she would get in touch with him after the funeral. Playing the good boyfriend, Max offered to attend the funeral with her, but she refused. She said that a few of her friends from work might be in attendance, and she could not afford the news of their relationship getting back to her boss and costing her her job. He understood and promised to be around when she was ready to talk or whatever.

In the midst of exchanging texts with Tia, one from Champagne squeezed its way in, and Max almost sent a text meant for Tia to Champagne. He concluded his previous text-chat and then proceeded to send a new one to his partner in crime.

She informed him of the key and the name of the nail salon where she was at, so he could come pick it up.

***

When Max left the salon, he swapped out his car for the Pacifica to do a little surveillance around Bonkerz before he made his move. The strip club was almost deserted in the early evening hour, so he did not park in the lot; instead, he parked in an alley that gave him a view of everything he needed to see. That was when he witnessed what he believed to be some type of illegal transaction going down in Bonkerz's parking lot. He saw two men he recognized as club bouncers unloading boxes from a moving truck into the back of a Dodge Durango.

It was pure curiosity that made Max follow the

suspicious-moving truck instead of the white Durango, since he already had a scheme in motion to hit Scrap. Following the truck, he ended up at the West Lawn Projects where two shady-looking Latinos got out of the blue Ford box truck and met with Kenny, a known drug dealer in the projects. They made the same exchange that Max had witnessed earlier; only this time the boxes were being loaded into a green Ford Windstar van. After the moving truck pulled away and Kenny went back inside the apartment, Max decided to get himself a bonus and steal the van just to see what was in the boxes.

Just like with the Camaro, he was inside the Windstar and gone in about a minute. Max pulled the van behind a school that was closed for the day. He then removed the three TV boxes that he saw the men cram into the van and stashed them in the school's dumpster.

He then drove the van within walking distance of where he left the Pacifica and ditched it by a crowded park. He quickly crossed the five city blocks on foot, hopped into the rental, retrieved the boxes, and headed over to Slugga's house, because it was closer, and he was anxious to see what was really inside the boxes.

"Let's see what you got here. I can tell ya one thing: they're crazy as hell if they think these cheap-ass TVs weigh this much," Slugga said, searching for the right bit for the drill.

"You gotta be the only nigga in the world who knows how heavy a damn television should be, 'cause I sure the hell couldn't tell you," Max responded, letting down the garage door so they could have some privacy.

Then he removed the other two televisions from the boxes. Max shook the last one to see if he could hear anything moving inside.

"Bro, you got your things and I got mine. Fooling with these electrical gadgets is what I do. That's why I'm the first person you niggas call when y'all get something new."

Slugga went to work removing the screws from the 65-inch flat screen. The television shell was so stuffed that it popped open before the last screw was completely out.

"My, my, my! Look at what they got on TV," Max said while lifting one of the pounds of weed from the hollowed-out television.

"Oh shit! This is my favorite show. I know one of these is mine, right?" Slugga asked, sniffing on one of the packages that he poked a hole in with the drill. "Ohhhhh, this is that fire, too. I gotta have two. There's one, three, five—there's like twenty of 'em in here!"

"Slugga, if it's the same thing in all of them, you can have ten. I don't give a fuck! This was some humbug shit for me. I'ma see if I can get a few of 'em off to Famous just to get it gone."

Slugga went to work opening the other

televisions, which all held the same amount in them.

“Bro, I can get four or five of them off for you right now. My white homie told me they lookin’ for some loud up where he at.”

“See if ya can dump all this shit off up there ‘cause I don’t got a line for it, and it’ll take me forever to get off with the few niggas I fuck with. So, yeah, do yo’ thang. Sell ‘em for like twenty-two each. I ain’t greedy,” Max told him, looking to make $88,000 off of the kush he was leaving with his friend.

Slugga quickly agreed, knowing he could make himself a nice profit off the price Max had given him. Max took ten pounds with him and drove straight home to put them up, so he could get back on his mission. On the way home, he decided to trade in the rental. He did not want to chance being seen in it after the two robberies he committed in it. He also decided not to mention the weed caper to Champagne since it really did not have anything to do with her.

Once back at home, Max received a text from Kake asking him for her usual ride, weed, and sex. It had been some time since they had hooked up, so he responded to her and let her know he would be there. Then the idea hit him to put some weed in Kake's hands to sell for him since she knew so many people that smoked.

On that note, Max held off from calling Famous, because he did not feel like explaining to him how he came about it. For all Max knew, Famous could be tight with Kenny and looking for someone trying to dump off large amounts of kush for the low, just like Max had intended to do before the idea to put it in Kake's hands.

Max rushed to the car rental office and traded in the Pacifica for a Dodge Journey. He then went back to his hiding place across from Bonkerz to continue his reconnaissance.

# CHAPTER 18

Playthang was doing her job in the office ironing the money nice and flat as promised. She started doing a little dance when she heard a song she liked coming through the walls from the strip club above them. Scrap paused what he was doing to watch her twerk. Playthang braced her hands on her knees while doing her dance. When she looked back over her shoulder, she caught him watching her ass wobble and shake, just like she wanted.

"What, is this shit boring? You act like you scared of me or something. You ain't said too much to me since Champ's been gone. What's up? I know you got questions—everyone does. So, go ahead and ask them," she told him while picking up the hot iron and poking her butt out to keep his attention.

"I just still can't believe what you are. I mean, how did you come to wanna be a bitch?" he asked, leaning back against the bar while arranging a stack of cash in his hand so that all the bills were facing the same direction.

"Well, mister man, believe it or not, I was born looking this fine. I haven't had any work done to my face. I look like my mom so much that it's sickening. I've always felt like a girl. I knew this is who I am meant to be, and as soon as I can get the rest of the money up I need, I'll be complete. The doctor I go to is really good, don't you think?" She grabbed his hand and pulled his arm around her hip. "He did my tits and ass. Feel it."

Scrap grabbed and squeezed her butt shamelessly.

"Yeah, he did a good job."

"No, dearie, he did a great job! Wait, let me take these off so you can get a better feel," she said before she stripped down to her underwear and then struck a sexy pose for him. "Now feel, and if ya make a little investment, I'll let you be the first one to test out my pussy after the procedure." She smiled.

"Bitch, you's a fool," he said smiling as he walked over to the desk and retrieved a CD case from the drawer. He opened the case and produced a small bag of cocaine. "Do you party?" he asked, dumping a nice quantity of the soft white work on the CD case, which now doubled as a plate.

After making five neat long lines of the work, Scrap dropped his face into the plate and snorted one of the lines before offering it to Playthang again.

"Hell yeah!" she said excitedly, quickly doing a line herself.

She tossed her head back as she handed it back over to him.

"Go ahead and do some more. You was the one talking about being so damn bored and shit. Let's liven things up in this muthafucka," he said.

He took the case, did another line, and then handed it back to her. Playthang knew if she kept going with it, she would not be able to finish Champagne's plan, so she did what she did best and started to dance. She was all over Scrap grinding her butt on him and kissing on his neck, all the while holding his hands out, so he could not touch her.

"If you wanna see me bust it open, it's going to cost you." She laughed when his eyes widened. "I'm just playing. You don't gotta pay me, daddy. You can have me however you want. But let's have some fun with all that cash in your hands."

She dropped down on the floor, lay on her back, and walked her legs up his body until she could feel his hard-on on the bottom of her feet.

Scrap pushed her long legs apart and grabbed another handful of cash.

"Work it for a nigga then. Yeah, work that muthafucka!"

He was really feeling the drug. Scrap held the money up high and let it fall, so it would sprinkle down on her.

"What the fuck is y'all doing?" Champagne snapped when she walked into the office on the private dance. "Bitch, get the fuck up! So is this why ya wanted to stay here and help so bad, bitch! What, bitch? Ya want my man?" Champagne pretended to charge at Playthang, who jumped up and behind Scrap.

"Champ, chill the fuck out! We wasn't doin' shit," he told her, holding her by the wrist as he pushed her away from Playthang. "You saw her dancin', and that's all she was doing. I told you I ain't on that. But it's okay for you to be dancin' all up on muthafuckas, but it's a fuckin' issue for a bitch to dance on me?"

"Fuck you, Scrap! Fuck you! If I wouldn't have walked in, this bitch right now would she still be just dancin', huh, nigga?" she yelled as she turned her focus on her friend. "Huh, bitch, would you?"

When Murdah's ringtone began playing on Scrap's cell, that's when he lost his patience with Champagne and slapped her.

"Bitch, if I tell you ain't shit going on, then ain't shit going on. Now get over there and sit the fuck down before I really get in yo' ass." He turned and picked up his phone from atop the minibar. "Play, put yo' shit back on and sit the fuck down with her. I ain't done with y'all yet," he said before he answered the call.

Playthang was about to protest, when she saw Champagne discreetly shaking her head no. She then flashed a devious smile before breaking down in tears. The act she was putting on could have won an award. Playthang rushed over to her friend's side and held her close.

"Champ, you're not mad at me for real, are you?" she asked in a whisper while hugging her.

"No, we good. In fact, let's get ready to kiss and make up when he gets off the phone. Just keep playing along," Champagne ordered her.

Scrap ended his call with Murdah. He then started putting things away as he explained to them that he had to go make a run, and he needed Champagne to stop tripping on them. She pulled away from Playthang and apologized for not trusting her, and then the two of them started making out in front of Scrap.

"See, now we all friends again, right?" he asked, walking up on them and placing his hands on their backs.

"No, you hit me, Scrap! Now you gotta kiss me so I feel better." Champagne pouted as she pulled him into the makeout session.

"Whoa, okay. Y'all, we gotta continue this later. I gotta go meet Murdah right now," he reminded them, pushing a wad of cash into their hands. "Y'all go shopping or some shit, and make sure ya come back with a good understanding of y'all's relationship. I'ma need you to finish helping me with this, and for ya to be on board with it like ya was at first."

Champagne took the money and agreed with him, while Playthang went and got dressed. That's when Champagne received a text from Max telling her he was coming to the club later. It was all coming together for her now, and this little bit of money Scrap had given her would be nothing compared to what she and Max would take from him soon, she thought smiling.

***To order books, please fill out the order form below:***
***To order films please go to www.good2gofilms.com***

Name: __ ______________________________

Address:______________________________

City: ____________ State: ______ Zip Code: ____________

Phone:______________________________

Email:______________________________

Method of Payment: Check VISA MASTERCARD

Credit Card#:_ ______________________________

Name as it appears on card: ______________________________

Signature: ______________________________

| Item Name | Price | Qty | Amount |
|---|---|---|---|
| 48 Hours to Die – Silk White | $14.99 | | |
| A Hustler's Dream - Ernest Morris | $14.99 | | |
| A Hustler's Dream 2 - Ernest Morris | $14.99 | | |
| A Thug's Devotion – J. L. Rose and J. M. McMillon | $14.99 | | |
| All Eyes on Tommy Gunz – Warren Holloway | $14.99 | | |
| Black Reign – Ernest Morris | $14.99 | | |
| Bloody Mayhem Down South – Trayvon Jackson | $14.99 | | |
| Bloody Mayhem Down South 2 – Trayvon Jackson | $14.99 | | |
| Business Is Business – Silk White | $14.99 | | |
| Business Is Business 2 – Silk White | $14.99 | | |
| Business Is Business 3 – Silk White | $14.99 | | |
| Cash In Cash Out – Assa Raymond Baker | $14.99 | | |
| Cash In Cash Out 2 - Assa Raymond Baker | $14.99 | | |
| Childhood Sweethearts – Jacob Spears | $14.99 | | |
| Childhood Sweethearts 2 – Jacob Spears | $14.99 | | |
| Childhood Sweethearts 3 - Jacob Spears | $14.99 | | |
| Childhood Sweethearts 4 - Jacob Spears | $14.99 | | |
| Connected To The Plug – Dwan Marquis Williams | $14.99 | | |
| Connected To The Plug 2 – Dwan Marquis Williams | $14.99 | | |
| Connected To The Plug 3 – Dwan Williams | $14.99 | | |
| Deadly Reunion – Ernest Morris | $14.99 | | |
| Dream's Life – Assa Raymond Baker | $14.99 | | |
| Flipping Numbers – Ernest Morris | $14.99 | | |
| Flipping Numbers 2 – Ernest Morris | $14.99 | | |
| He Loves Me, He Loves You Not - Mychea | $14.99 | | |
| He Loves Me, He Loves You Not 2 - Mychea | $14.99 | | |
| He Loves Me, He Loves You Not 3 - Mychea | $14.99 | | |

| | | | |
|---|---|---|---|
| He Loves Me, He Loves You Not 4 – Mychea | $14.99 | | |
| He Loves Me, He Loves You Not 5 – Mychea | $14.99 | | |
| Lord of My Land – Jay Morrison | $14.99 | | |
| Lost and Turned Out – Ernest Morris | $14.99 | | |
| Love Hates Violence – De'Wayne Maris | $14.99 | | |
| Married To Da Streets – Silk White | $14.99 | | |
| M.E.R.C. - Make Every Rep Count Health and Fitness | $14.99 | | |
| Money Make Me Cum – Ernest Morris | $14.99 | | |
| My Besties – Asia Hill | $14.99 | | |
| My Besties 2 – Asia Hill | $14.99 | | |
| My Besties 3 – Asia Hill | $14.99 | | |
| My Besties 4 – Asia Hill | $14.99 | | |
| My Boyfriend's Wife - Mychea | $14.99 | | |
| My Boyfriend's Wife 2 – Mychea | $14.99 | | |
| My Brothers Envy – J. L. Rose | $14.99 | | |
| My Brothers Envy 2 – J. L. Rose | $14.99 | | |
| Naughty Housewives – Ernest Morris | $14.99 | | |
| Naughty Housewives 2 – Ernest Morris | $14.99 | | |
| Naughty Housewives 3 – Ernest Morris | $14.99 | | |
| Naughty Housewives 4 – Ernest Morris | $14.99 | | |
| Never Be The Same – Silk White | $14.99 | | |
| Shades of Revenge – Assa Raymond Baker | $14.99 | | |
| Slumped – Jason Brent | $14.99 | | |
| Someone's Gonna Get It – Mychea | $14.99 | | |
| Stranded – Silk White | $14.99 | | |
| Supreme & Justice – Ernest Morris | $14.99 | | |
| Supreme & Justice 2 – Ernest Morris | $14.99 | | |
| Supreme & Justice 3 – Ernest Morris | $14.99 | | |
| Tears of a Hustler - Silk White | $14.99 | | |
| Tears of a Hustler 2 - Silk White | $14.99 | | |
| Tears of a Hustler 3 - Silk White | $14.99 | | |
| Tears of a Hustler 4- Silk White | $14.99 | | |
| Tears of a Hustler 5 – Silk White | $14.99 | | |
| Tears of a Hustler 6 – Silk White | $14.99 | | |

| | | | |
|---|---|---|---|
| The Last Love Letter – Warren Holloway | $14.99 | | |
| The Last Love Letter 2 – Warren Holloway | $14.99 | | |
| The Panty Ripper - Reality Way | $14.99 | | |
| The Panty Ripper 3 – Reality Way | $14.99 | | |
| The Solution – Jay Morrison | $14.99 | | |
| The Teflon Queen – Silk White | $14.99 | | |
| The Teflon Queen 2 – Silk White | $14.99 | | |
| The Teflon Queen 3 – Silk White | $14.99 | | |
| The Teflon Queen 4 – Silk White | $14.99 | | |
| The Teflon Queen 5 – Silk White | $14.99 | | |
| The Teflon Queen 6 - Silk White | $14.99 | | |
| The Vacation – Silk White | $14.99 | | |
| Tied To A Boss - J.L. Rose | $14.99 | | |
| Tied To A Boss 2 - J.L. Rose | $14.99 | | |
| Tied To A Boss 3 - J.L. Rose | $14.99 | | |
| Tied To A Boss 4 - J.L. Rose | $14.99 | | |
| Tied To A Boss 5 - J.L. Rose | $14.99 | | |
| Time Is Money - Silk White | $14.99 | | |
| Tomorrow's Not Promised – Robert Torres | $14.99 | | |
| Tomorrow's Not Promised 2 – Robert Torres | $14.99 | | |
| Two Mask One Heart – Jacob Spears and Trayvon Jackson | $14.99 | | |
| Two Mask One Heart 2 – Jacob Spears and Trayvon Jackson | $14.99 | | |
| Two Mask One Heart 3 – Jacob Spears and Trayvon Jackson | $14.99 | | |
| Wrong Place Wrong Time – Silk White | $14.99 | | |
| Young Goonz – Reality Way | $14.99 | | |
| | | | |
| Subtotal: | | | |
| Tax: | | | |
| Shipping (Free) U.S. Media Mail: | | | |
| Total: | | | |

**Make Checks Payable To:**
**Good2Go Publishing**
**7311 W Glass Lane,**
**Laveen, AZ 85339**